A

"Hand over the money," said the man in the middle.

"What money?" Ike asked. "We don't have any money."

"We wuz told different."

"Really?" Clint asked. "By who?"

"That don't matter."

Clint looked around them, beyond them, into the shadows. He thought he saw someone, watching. He thought he knew who it was. Somebody who was interested in standing back and watching, seeing what he had left.

These men were a sacrifice.

"You don't want to do this," he said to them.

"Why not?" the middle man, Rango, asked.

"Because we might be carrying money," Clint said, "but it's not enough for all of you to die for."

"Hey," one of the other men said, "who is this guy? He thinks he can kill five of us?"

"He knows he can," Ike said.

"Whataya mean, he knows he can?" Rango asked. "How can he know that?"

"Because," Ike said, "his name is Clint Adams."

All five men stared at Clint.

"You know," Ike continued, "the Gunsmith?"

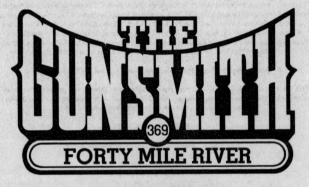

THE GUNSMITH

369

FORTY MILE RIVER

J. R. ROBERTS

JOVE BOOKS, NEW YORK

THE BERKLEY PUBLISHING GROUP
Published by the Penguin Group
Penguin Group (USA) Inc.
375 Hudson Street, New York, New York 10014, USA

Penguin Group (Canada), 90 Eglinton Avenue East, Suite 700, Toronto, Ontario M4P 2Y3, Canada
(a division of Pearson Penguin Canada Inc.) • Penguin Books Ltd., 80 Strand, London WC2R 0RL,
England • Penguin Group Ireland, 25 St. Stephen's Green, Dublin 2, Ireland (a division of Penguin
Books Ltd.) • Penguin Group (Australia), 250 Camberwell Road, Camberwell, Victoria 3124, Australia
(a division of Pearson Australia Group Pty. Ltd.) • Penguin Books India Pvt. Ltd., 11 Community
Centre, Panchsheel Park, New Delhi—110 017, India • Penguin Group (NZ), 67 Apollo Drive,
Rosedale, Auckland 0632, New Zealand (a division of Pearson New Zealand Ltd.) • Penguin Books
(South Africa) (Pty.) Ltd., 24 Sturdee Avenue, Rosebank, Johannesburg 2196, South Africa

Penguin Books Ltd., Registered Offices: 80 Strand, London WC2R 0RL, England

This is a work of fiction. Names, characters, places, and incidents either are the product of the author's
imagination or are used fictitiously, and any resemblance to actual persons, living or dead, business
establishments, events, or locales is entirely coincidental.

FORTY MILE RIVER

A Jove Book / published by arrangement with the author

PUBLISHING HISTORY
Jove edition / September 2012

Copyright © 2012 by Robert J. Randisi.
Cover illustration by Sergio Giovine.

ISBN: 978-0-515-15109-1

JOVE®
Jove Books are published by The Berkley Publishing Group,
a division of Penguin Group (USA) Inc.,
375 Hudson Street, New York, New York 10014.
JOVE® is a registered trademark of Penguin Group (USA) Inc.
The "J" design is a trademark of Penguin Group (USA) Inc.

PRINTED IN THE UNITED STATES OF AMERICA

1 2 3 4 5 6 7 8 9 10

ALWAYS LEARNING   **PEARSON**

ONE

Clint heard the deck creak outside his room.

If he had been in a hotel, it would have meant someone was walking in the hall outside his room. But on a steamship like the *Lady Gay*, all it meant was that the deck was creaking.

The *Lady Gay*, owned by the West Coast Steamship Company, out of Seattle, was heading to Alaska. The discovery of gold had caused people to flock there to pan or dig for their fortune. Clint was on his way to see a friend, who said he already had a big claim and needed a partner. Since he had nothing on his plate, Clint decided to go ahead and make the trip north. It had been years since he'd been in Alaska.

The girl in bed with him rolled over and looked at him.

"I could feel you were awake," she said.

"Well, I tried not to wake you, but I can't do anything about *that*."

"Yes, you can." She scooted over to him, plastering

her hot, naked body against his. "You can make it up to me. Or are you thinking about playing poker?"

"Actually, I wasn't," he said. "I was thinking about this ship, and where we're headed."

"Alaska?"

"Skagway, more specifically," he said. "And beyond."

"I'm only heading for Skagway," she said. "Where are you going?"

"North of there, about fifteen hundred miles."

"Jesus," she said. "How are you gonna get there? And why?"

"A boat, on the river," he said, "and for gold."

"You don't look like a man who has gold fever," she said.

"I don't," he said, "but I'm meeting up with a man who just might."

"A friend?"

He nodded.

"You'd go that far for a friend?"

He put his arms around her and said, "I guess that's my one big flaw."

"You only have one?"

She snuggled closer to him and said, "It's going to get colder the closer we get."

"Too cold for sex?"

She kissed his chest and said, "Never too cold for that. At least, not if we stay under the covers."

They had a sheet and a blanket on them, and combined with her body heat, they were extremely warm.

"I'm so glad not to be up on deck," she said.

Clint had been lucky enough to get a cabin on board. There were so many passengers that the deck was overcrowded with them, many of them sleeping in bedrolls, or simply on blankets rolled out on the deck. He had felt a little guilty about it, but not any longer. At least he was sharing his bed and cabin with Frankie.

Her name was Francesca Morgan, but as soon as they had met up on deck, she'd told him to call her Frankie. He had invited her into the lounge with him, where they had dinner and then he played some poker while she watched. She had gotten her ticket at the last minute and had only been able to get deck space. She was very happy to be inside, and he was just as happy to help her. When it got late, he asked her if she wanted to sleep in his cabin. She readily agreed. After that, nature had just taken its course.

That initial meeting had taken place the first day, and she had been sharing his cabin—and his bed—ever since then.

He rolled her onto her back and she wrapped her legs around him . . .

In another part of the ship, two men sat at the bar in the lounge. Around them, men sat at tables, some playing poker, others just drinking. They had all been able to afford paying for the right, unlike the teeming masses who were crowded onto the deck.

Actually, the *Lady Gay* was not meant to carry passengers. The holds of the ship were packed with supplies that would be used to dig gold out of the hard-packed earth in Alaska.

But where there's a will to make money, there's a way. So the hold was filled with supplies, and the deck was filled with paying passengers. And some of the passengers had paid enough for a lounge to be set up, and to have cabins.

Calvin Parker was such a man. The man with him was his assistant, Hector Tailor.

"Sir, there's something I don't understand," Hector said.

"Then ask, Hector," Parker said. "I want you to understand every aspect of your job. If you have questions, ask them."

"You have the money to finance this operation," Calvin said. "I mean, you have more money than any ten men I've ever known. Why go all the way to Alaska?"

"Because," Parker said, "that's where the gold is. And because, for me, it's unconquered territory."

"Is that what it's about for you, then?" Hector asked. "Exploring the unconquered?"

"It's more than that, Hector. It's about conquering the unconquered," Parker said. "That's what it's about for all great men."

Hector studied his boss while the man drank down most of his brandy. He didn't think he was looking at a great man—not yet anyway. But he was looking at a man who was going to pay him a lot of money, so he raised his own glass.

"Here's to great men," he said.

Parker raised his own glass in response and said, "Here's to a great man."

TWO

Clint nuzzled Francesca's breasts, teasing the dark brown nipples until they were fully turgid in his mouth.

She moaned, held his head in her arms, pressing him to her, but he wasn't satisfied to stay there. He worked his way down her body, trying to make sure the covers didn't slide off them. He kissed her belly, licked her belly button, then buried his nose in that hairy, fragrant V between her thighs.

He probed there with his tongue until he found her already slick and wet, and then went to work with his tongue and his lips until she was bouncing around on the bed in such a frenzy that the covers went flying to the floor.

"Oh, my God!" she cried, reaching down not to hold him there, but to push him away. "You're going to kill me!"

Finally he allowed her to push him away, but just

so he could mount her and drive himself into her. His penis was like a column of stone and she gasped as he entered her.

She wrapped her legs around him once more, and he marveled again that, for a slender girl, she had very strong thighs.

He slid his hands beneath her to cup her smooth ass and then proceeded to fuck her hard and fast because— after many days together—he knew this was what she liked. He preferred something slower, but eventually he got what he wanted, too.

They were a good match. It was too bad the voyage would soon come to an end . . .

"So you're really heading up the river when we get to Skagway?" she asked. They were back under the covers, and she was lying wrapped in his arms.

"As soon as we get there," he said. "First day. My friend should be waiting there for me."

"Do you know how many days that trip will take?" she asked.

"No," he said, "but I'll find out."

"Can't you stay in Skagway just for a while?" she asked.

"I'm afraid not," Clint said. "I'm going to be a slave to my friend's schedule."

"He must be a very good friend."

"He is," Clint said, although he thought a trip to Alaska, and time spent up the river, might put that to the test.

He held her tightly until she fell asleep, then allowed

her to roll off him to the other side of the bed. He stood up, pulled on his clothes, and went up on deck for some air.

"You know the Gunsmith is on board?" Hector asked his boss.

"Clint Adams? That's interesting. How do you know that?"

"I saw him."

"You know him on sight?"

"Yes, sir," Hector said. "I saw him once in Kansas City."

"Saw him do what?"

"Kill three men."

"In the street?"

"Yes, sir."

"Alone?"

"Yes, just him against them. He outdrew them cleanly. None of them even got off a shot."

"How long ago was that?"

"Three years."

Parker looked into his third brandy of the night.

"Wonder why he's going to Alaska," he said aloud, even though he was really asking himself the question.

"Why does anybody go to Alaska?" Hector asked. "Gold."

"But the Gunsmith?" Parker said. "I've never heard anything about him being greedy."

"You think only greedy men go after gold?"

"Well, of course," Parker said. "Come on, Hector.

You just pointed out that I have a lot of money. What reason other than greed could cause me to go to Alaska for gold?"

"Yes, but—"

"There's nothing wrong with greed, son," Parker said. "Nothing at all. Learn to be greedy and you might make something of yourself."

Parker finished his third brandy, then set the glass down and left the lounge. He didn't go out onto the deck, but rather used the door that would lead him belowdecks, to his cabin.

Hector thought about what his boss had said, then turned to the bartender and ordered a beer.

THREE

Once he was out on deck, Clint started to think he'd made a mistake. He could have gotten to the lounge without going on deck, but he wanted some air. Now he was getting hard looks from the people who had to sleep on deck during this whole trip. Wrapped in their blankets and bedrolls, they recognized him as somebody who had a cabin. Clint almost felt the need to apologize as he walked among them and eventually reached the lounge.

Inside it was quiet, with the sound of glasses clinking and chips falling. Clint walked to the lounge, where a few men were standing, and ordered a beer.

"Comin' up," the bartender said.

"Mr. Adams's beer will be on me," a young man said from down the bar.

"Much obliged," Clint said.

"Do you mind if I join you?" the man asked.

"Not at all," Clint said.

The man grabbed his own beer and walked down to where Clint was standing.

"My name is Tailor, Hector Tailor."

Clint shook the man's hand and said, "You seem to know who I am."

"Indeed I do," Hector said. "I saw you once in Kansas City."

"I've been to Kansas City many times," Clint said as the bartender set his beer down on the bar. "Which time are you referring to?"

"I saw you kill three men in the street in a fair fight," Hector said.

"Ah," Clint said, "that was about three years back. Not my finest hour."

"But . . . you were magnificent!"

"Believe it or not, Mr. Tailor—"

"Hector, please."

"Believe it or not, Hector, I try not to kill people," Clint explained.

"I . . . well . . . your reputation . . ."

"You can't always believe a man's reputation."

"I'm . . . sorry. I shouldn't have—"

"Don't worry about it," Clint said. "Let's drink up and then I'll buy you one."

They talked for a while, as Hector tried to discover what was taking the Gunsmith to Alaska.

He told Clint that he was traveling with his boss, who was going to be setting up a mining operation in Alaska. There was no harm in telling him this, because it was all true.

"What's taking you there?" he asked then.

"What's taking everyone there?" Clint asked. "All those people crowded onto the decks?"

"Gold? But . . . you don't strike me as the kind of man who would be enticed by gold."

"I'm not," Clint said, "but I know somebody who is, and he sent me a telegram."

"And on the strength of that, you're going to Alaska?" Hector asked. "This must be some friend."

"Yes," Clint said, "yes, he's a good friend."

"Well, I wish you both luck," Hector said. "Does he have a claim already?"

"I assume so, but I really don't know," Clint said. "I won't know until I get there."

"Wow," Hector said, "you are a good friend."

They finished their beer and Clint bought them each another one.

"And your boss?" Clint asked. "He has a claim?"

"Oh, yes," Hector said. "A large one. He has equipment in the hold of the ship."

"So he's setting up a major mining concern."

"Oh, yes, major."

"What's his name?"

"Calvin Parker."

"Hmm, Calvin? I don't know that name."

"Well, maybe you will once he gets set up," Hector said. "I think I'm going to turn in, Clint. It was real nice meeting you."

"Yeah, Hector, you, too."

"Maybe we'll see each other in Skagway."

"I hope so," Clint said. "I'd like to meet your boss."

"I'm sure he'd like to meet you, too."

As Hector left, Clint finished his beer and ordered another one.

"You have any idea when we'll get to Skagway?" he asked the bartender.

"Can't be too soon for me," the man said. "I'm lookin' to get off this boat."

"Yeah, I guess you spend a lot of time on here."

"Yeah, too much," he said. "And I don't wanna be here when all those people on deck decide to take over."

"You think that's going to happen?"

"Oh, yeah. Each time we make this trip, I'm waitin' for them to get fed up. It'll happen."

"So do you know?" Clint asked.

"Know what?"

"When we'll be getting to Skagway?"

The man thought a moment, then said, "Can't be too soon for me."

"Right."

FOUR

Clint was on deck with Frankie several days later when Skagway came into view. It was teeming with people, on its streets, on the docks, on the beaches. He didn't know how all the people on the ship were going to fit. He was glad Ike Daly would be meeting him at the dock and that he wouldn't have to stay in Skagway more than a few hours.

The dock was foggy with the frosted breath of the passengers. The mountains beyond the town were covered with snow. There were chunks of ice floating in the water.

"Is someone meeting you at the dock?" he asked Frankie.

"Oh, yes."

"I'll stay with you until you find them."

One of the crewmen was waving to Clint, so he and Frankie made their way through the crush of bodies until they reached him.

"The captain says you kin get off with the first wave, Mr. Adams."

"She comes with me," Clint said.

"No skin off my nose," the crewman said. "And I can't say as I blame ya. Go ahead."

Clint and Frankie disembarked with the others who'd had the good fortune to obtain cabins. Among them were Hector Tailor and his boss, Calvin Parker.

"Mr. Tailor," Clint said as they walked down the gangplank.

"Mr. Adams," Hector said. "This is my boss, Mr. Parker."

"Mr. Adams, glad to meet you," Parker said.

"This is Miss Francesca Morgan," Clint said.

"Miss Morgan," Parker said politely. He then looked at Clint. "Hector tells me you won't be in Skagway very long."

"No, sir."

"Long enough for me to buy you a drink, or a meal?" Parker asked.

"I don't know," Clint said. "That will depend on my friend."

"Well, we'll be staying at the Skagway Hotel," Parker said. "If you've got the time, come by and we'll eat together."

"I appreciate the offer, Mr. Parker. Thank you."

"And by all means, bring the lovely lady," Parker said.

When they reached the bottom of the gangplank, they were literally swept away in different directions.

"Frankie!" a woman's voice called out. "Frankie, over here!"

They both looked in the direction of the voice and saw a small young woman waving her arms. They moved toward her. Clint noticed she was cleaner than most of the people around her.

When they reached her, she smiled and asked, "Are you Frankie?" It became apparent to Clint that she had simply been calling Frankie's name, hoping to be heard.

"That's right."

"I'm Lindy. Come with me, then," the woman said. "We have to get you set up. It's nickel night." She looked at Clint. "Is this your man?"

"No," Frankie said, "just a friend I met on the ship."

"Well, say good-bye, then," Lindy said. "We got to go."

Frankie looked at Clint, and he could see she was hoping he had not interpreted the conversation correctly.

"Take care, Francesca," he said.

She kissed his cheek and said, "Good luck, Clint."

As Lindy drew her off into the crowd, Clint thought she was the one who was going to need luck. There was only one way to interpret "nickel night."

FIVE

"Clint!"

He turned and saw Ike Daly coming toward him. Unlike Lindy, he did not seem to be cleaner than the people around him. In fact, if anything, he was the dirtiest man on the docks.

"Hey, Ike!"

Daly charged him and grabbed him in a bear hug, which hurt. Ike Daly was six-feet-four, weight well over two hundred pounds. But something in the hug was lacking, and Daly looked to Clint to have dropped some weight.

When he put him down, Clint asked, "You been sick?"

"Ah, I been a bit poorly," Daly said, "but that's gonna change now that yer here. Jesus, I didn't think you'd really come."

"I sent you a telegram and you're here to meet me," Clint said.

"Oh, yeah, I know, but I still—aw, forget it. Come on, let's get a drink."

"I thought we were leaving as soon as we got here," Clint said.

"We are, we are, but first we gotta talk about a few things."

"Like what?"

"Come on, let's get a—"

"Like what, Ike? Money?"

"Well . . . that's one thing."

"You got unpaid bills?"

"Don't everybody got unpaid bills, Clint?"

"I don't."

"Well, you also don't own nothin'," Ike pointed out. "Except a horse. You bring your horse?"

"No, I left him in Seattle."

"That's probably a good thing. By the time we got where we're goin' on horseback, them animals would be dead. We're goin' by boat."

"I figured."

"But first . . ."

"Yeah?"

"We gotta buy some boats."

Clint stared at his friend and shook his head.

"Yeah, okay," he said.

Clint was shivering and said, "I need to get someplace warm."

"Oh, yeah," Ike said, "I brung you this." He handed Clint a fur-lined jacket.

"Hey, thanks." Clint slipped it on, and was immediately warmer.

"Okay," Ike said, "let's go get a drink."

* * *

Calvin Parker and Hector Tailor watched as the steve-
dores unloaded their supplies from the hold of the ship,
and loaded them onto wagons on the dock.

"Do we have reliable men to deliver this stuff?"
Parker asked Hector.

"Yes, sir. They've made the trip before."

"And we're going by boat?"

"That's right."

"Who will get there first?"

"We should beat them there."

"Good," Parker said. "I want to supervise the unloading of the supplies."

"Would you like to go to the hotel now?"

"Yes, I would."

"Good," Hector said. "This cold is freezing my toes."

"I'm going to the hotel," Parker said, "but you're not."

"Sir?"

"You stay here until all the supplies are loaded and
these wagons are on their way," Parker said. "Then come
to the hotel to have dinner with me. Understand?"

"Yes, sir."

"Good," Parker said. "Do a good job, Hector, like
you always do."

"Yes, sir."

"And if you see Adams, your new friend," Parker
said, "see if you can find out exactly where he's going.
And if it's anywhere near where we're going."

"Yes, sir."

Parker started to walk away, then stopped. "Oh, yeah,
and find me somebody good with a gun."

"Good with a gun . . . how?"

"Good," Parker said. "Fast, accurate, and—oh, yeah—it would help if he's already killed a few men."

"So you want a gunman," Hector said.

"That's what I want," Parker said. "A gunman, a gunfighter, a killer, whatever you want to call it. Just get me one."

"Yes, sir."

"And bring him to dinner."

"Tonight?" Hector said. "You want me to find him . . . tonight?"

"That's what I said, Hector," Parker replied. "Tonight. Do you still understand me?"

"I do, yes, sir."

"Okay, then," Parker said. "See you both tonight for dinner."

Hector watched his boss walk away, then turned just as some of his boss's equipment fell from the ship to the dock.

SIX

The saloon Ike took Clint to was as packed with people as the deck of the ship had been.

"Get that table," Ike said. "That one there! I'll get the beer."

Miraculously, the table had opened up and Clint was able to grab it. It was a rough-hewn table for two, with two rickety chairs. Ike came over and fell into the other chair, set the two beers down without spilling a drop.

"One thing about Alaska," he said.

"What's that?"

"The beer's always cold."

Clint sipped it and found that an understatement. The beer was like ice.

Ike drank half of it down and then grimaced as the cold moved into his head.

"Wow," he said. "That's good."

"Okay, Ike," Clint said. "Talk."

"Look," Ike said, "I'm just a little short of cash for the boats."

"The boats."

"And the men to man the poles."

"Poles?"

"Poles," Ike said. "It's the only way to negotiate these rivers in a flat bottom boat."

"Jesus," Clint said, "how long is this trip going to take?"

"Not as long as if we tried to take everything by wagon, over the mountains."

"So we'll get there at the same time our supplies do."

"Yes."

"How many men are we hiring?"

"Four."

"Just for the ride?"

"No, we can use them when we get there, too," Ike said.

"And do you already have men there working?"

"Oh, yeah," Ike said. "Don't worry. The gold is being pulled from the ground even as we sit here and drink."

"Ike—"

"I swear, Clint," Ike said. "We're both gonna get rich."

"But first you need my money."

"Uh . . . yeah."

"How much?"

Ike told him. "It's really not that much," he insisted. "I mean, considering what we're gonna get—"

"Relax, relax," Clint said. "I've got it."

"The money?"

Clint nodded.

"I figured it was going to cost me as soon as I got here," Clint said, "and I also figured we were going to spend lot of time not near a town or a bank."

"And who would try to rob the Gunsmith, right?" Ike asked. "You can carry as much money with you as you want."

"And if you keep your voice down," Clint pointed out, "nobody else will start asking themselves that same question."

"I get it," Ike said.

"So okay, what's next?"

"We'll meet with the men and pay them half their money," Ike said. "They'll get the other half when we get to our camp."

"And they're okay with that?"

"As long as they get half up front, yeah."

"So when do we leave? Tonight?"

"In the morning."

"I wasn't planning on staying the night," Clint said. "Are there rooms?"

"I have a room at the Skagway for both of us."

"To share?"

"Don't worry," Ike said. "There's two beds."

Clint sniffed his friend and said, "I wasn't worried about the number of beds. Do they have bathtubs?"

"I think they do. Why? You need a bath?"

"I wasn't thinking about me."

Hector Tailor had a specialty that made him the perfect assistant. He had contacts. You would think his contacts would make him the ideal boss, but he lacked the ambition—and courage—for that. Oh, he had enough courage to go into the darkest corners, but to be the man responsible for everything? No.

"You want Bent Miller," his contact, Willie Cotton, told him.

"How do I find him?" Hector asked.

"You don't. I do. Where do you want him to meet you?"

"The Skagway Hotel."

"You'll have to pay him."

"I assumed that."

"No, I mean you'll have to pay him just to listen," Cotton said.

"That's okay," Hector said, "but it has to be tonight. And we'll feed him."

"I'll let him know. He also has some . . . colleagues. Would you be needing them?"

"If we do, we'll talk to him about it."

"Fine," Cotton said. "I'll do what I can."

Hector handed him some money—more than the little man had asked for.

"I'll do my best," he promised.

"You do that."

When Ike let Clint into the room, Clint eyed the two rickety beds dubiously. They were hardly as big as the pallets found in most jail cells.

"This was the best we could do," Ike said.

"It's only going to be one night, right?"

"That's right."

Clint dropped his carpetbag on the bed, surprised that it didn't collapse beneath the weight.

"Okay," he said, turning to Ike, "now about that bath . . ."

SEVEN

After they each had a bath, Ike took Clint back onto the crowded streets of Skagway. They walked a few blocks to a small café.

"It's cheap, but it's good," Ike said as they stood out front.

Clint could smell burnt meat, among other things, coming from inside.

"I don't usually go cheap on my food, Ike," he said. "You been eating here the whole time?"

"Only been here a week, but yeah, pretty much."

"Okay," Clint said, "well, do you know anyplace better than this, where they don't burn the meat?"

"Sure, there are a couple of places we could go."

"Well, pick one out," Clint said. "Don't worry about the money—not when it comes to food."

"Okay, then," Ike said, "we might as well go to the best place in town."

"We might as well," Clint agreed.

*   *   *

Calvin Parker looked up from his steak, saw Hector Tailor enter the restaurant alone. He'd been given the name of this place by his assistant, who had gotten it from his contact as a place to get a good steak. At least, in that respect, Hector had gotten something right.

"Thought I told you to bring him with you tonight," Parker said.

"He'll be here," Hector said. "He's supposed to meet us."

"Supposed to?"

"He'll meet us."

"He'd better," Parker said, "or you'll be on the next boat back to Seattle." He waved over a waiter. "Bring my friend what he wants."

"I'll have a steak," Hector said, "well done."

"Well done," Parker said, shaking his head. "Jesus, why don't you tell them to burn it."

"I don't like all that blood on my plate," Hector said.

"That's your problem, Hector," Parker said. "You're too squeamish about blood. When is this fella going to turn up?"

"Any minute."

"What's his name?"

"Bent Miller."

"Bent?"

Hector shrugged.

"My contact says we'll have to feed him and pay him, and that's just to listen."

"Is that a fact?"

"Yes, sir."

"Well, we'll see."

Hector looked around. Most of the diners seemed to be eating the same thing—steak dinners. That explained why the waiter appeared almost immediately with his. Seemed they had steaks cooking in the kitchen all the time.

"You told him about this place?" Parker asked.

"He knows," Hector assured him as the waiter set his plate down in front of him.

"Then eat your steak, Hector," Parker said. "If this man Bent doesn't show up, that'll be the last meal you have on me."

"Yes, sir."

Bent Miller stopped in front of the River Steakhouse. He'd eaten there once and had found it very good. He was looking forward to eating there again, especially with someone else paying the freight.

"Come on," Ed Stash said. "Let's go eat."

"Yeah," Billy Rohm said. "I always wanted to eat here."

"Hold it!" Bent Miller said.

Both men froze.

"I'm eatin' here," Bent said, "you ain't."

"What?"

"Yeah," Bent said, "go and find someplace else to eat, and meet me here in a half an hour. By then I'll know if we have a job."

"This ain't fair!" Rohm complained.

"So what?" Bent said. "Life ain' never been fair to us, has it?"

"Got that right," Stash said.

"Go!" Bent said. "Get outta here."

The two men slunk off to eat, as usual, in some flea-infested restaurant.

Bent Miller approached the River Steakhouse, which was housed in one of the first wooden structures that had been built in Skagway. As he entered, he immediately spotted and recognized the two men he was supposed to meet.

EIGHT

"This has to be him," Parker said, looking past Hector at the man who had just come through the door.

Hector turned, saw a dangerous-looking man standing just inside the door. He was dressed warmly in a fur-lined jacket, had a well-worn Colt in a holster on his hip, his lantern jaw covered with gray-black stubble.

"Just because he looks dangerous?" Hector asked.

"Because," Calvin Parker said, "he looks like a killer."

"How can you tell?"

"Easy," Parker said. "The eyes. It's always in the eyes."

"I guess I better—"

"Just sit tight," Parker said, cutting him off before he could say anything else. "Let him pick us out. You gave a description, right?"

"Right."

"Then just wait."

Hector turned and went back to his steak.

* * *

Bent Miller knew tenderfeet when he saw them. He walked over to the table, stopped just behind Hector Tailor, and dropped his hand on his shoulder.

"You're Tailor," he said.

Hector looked over his shoulder, and up.

"That's right," he said. "Bent Miller, right?"

"That's right."

"Well, sit down and have a steak," Hector said.

"I have a fee coming first," Bent said.

"This is my boss, Calvin Parker," Hector said. "He has your fee."

"Mr. Parker," Bent said.

"Mr. Miller," Parker said. "I believe your fee was a steak and . . ."

"A thousand dollars."

"A thousand?" Parker asked. "Why do I think it's more like . . . five hundred?"

Hector wondered why Parker was negotiating, but Bent Miller looked at him and said, "Yeah, five hundred. That's it."

Parker took some money out of his pocket and set it down by the third chair, then waved to the waiter to bring another steak dinner.

"The River," Ike said.

"We're going to go and eat in the river?" Clint asked.

"No," Ike said, "we're going to a steakhouse called the River. Serves the best steak in Skagway. There it is."

Clint found himself looking at a shack.

"That's the best place in town for steak?"

"It's also one of the first buildings ever built in Skagway."

As they approached, Clint could see inside.

"Looks pretty busy."

"Every place in Skagway is busy," Ike said. "Come on."

They walked to the door and went inside. Just from the crush of bodies present it was warmer.

"I see a table in the back," Ike said.

"Well, hurry up," Clint said. "I'm hungry."

Ike ran across the floor to claim the table as two people stood up from it. Clint started to follow, then saw three men sitting at a table together. He recognized two of them as Hector Tailor and Calvin Parker. He didn't know the third man, but he certainly was not cut from the same cloth as the two businessmen.

By the time he reached the table, Ike had cleared it off with his sleeve and waved to a waiter.

"Two steak dinners," he said. "And beer."

"Comin' up."

Ike looked over at the table of three men that had caught Clint's eye.

"You know them fellers?" he asked.

"I know two of them," Clint said. "Came over on the ship with me. I don't know the third."

"I do," Ike said. "That's Bent Miller."

"Who's Bent Miller?" Clint asked.

"He's the man you hire when you need a gun," Ike said. "Him and his partners kill for a livin'."

"That so?" Clint asked. "I wonder what two businessmen need with a killer, just hours after they've arrived here in Alaska."

"What's their business here?" Ike asked.

"What else? Gold. Apparently, the one with the mustache, Calvin Parker, has a lot of money and is planning on setting up a mining operation."

"Where?"

"I don't know," Clint said.

"Well," Ike said, "I hope it ain't up near Forty Mile."

"Forty Mile?"

"That's the town we're headin' for," Ike said, "and we're takin' Forty Mile River to get there."

"And it's a town?"

"Shanty town mostly," Ike said. "May've grown since I was there, but there's plenty of folks headin' up that way."

"There should be enough gold for everybody," Clint said.

"That ain't the attitude of everybody up here," Ike said. "In fact, it ain't hardly anybody's attitude. Nobody's lookin' to share nothin'."

"That can only lead to trouble," Clint said.

The waiter came with their plates and set them down in front of them, then came back with two frosty beers. Ike grabbed his and drank a quarter of it down.

"Too many damn people here for you to hand me any money," Ike said around a huge chunk of steak. "Maybe we should wait 'til we get to the hotel."

"I'll pass the cash to you under the table," Clint suggested. "Don't you have to pay it out right away? Tonight?"

"Soon as I can," Ike said. "I wanna make sure our stuff hits the river early tomorrow."

"Are we goin' on the same boat?"

"No," Ike said. "The supplies will go up on a couple

of boats. We'll go on a separate one. With three boats, we're gonna need a lot of men on the poles."

"How bad is the river between here and there?"

"There's some bad spots, but it should be smooth as glass most of the way."

"Are the men you're hiring experienced?"

"Very," Ike said. "That's why I need so much money."

"So much?"

"Well, I ain't payin' them each a lot, but it adds up."

"Seems to me these fellas would be in demand," Clint said. "Especially with somebody like Calvin Parker in town."

"You're right," Ike said. "That's why I gotta get 'em paid tonight."

"Well, okay, then," Clint said. "I'll pass you the cash under the table."

"But you got more, right?"

"I brought enough to get the job done, Ike," Clint said.

"That's good," Ike said. "Let's eat up and then we can get to it."

NINE

Calvin Parker was looking over at Clint and the other man.

"Hector, do you know who that man with Adams is?" he asked.

"No, sir, I don't."

"Well, find out—"

"He don't have to," Bent Miller said, chewing his steak. "I know who he is."

"Okay," Parker said, "who?"

"Ike Daly."

"Who is he?"

"Small operator," Bent said. "But did you say that other fella's name is Adams?"

"That's right," Parker said. "Clint Adams, the Gunsmith."

"So that's why you need me?" Bent asked.

"Maybe," Parker said. "I just want to be ready if Adams plans to get in my way."

"I can take care of him right here in Skagway, no problem," Bent said.

"You're that confident?" Hector asked.

"Oh, yeah," Bent said. "He's got some time on him, ain't what he used to be. Me, I'm younger and faster, and probably meaner. Oh, yeah, I can do it."

"Let's just hold off on that, Miller," Parker said.

"Just call me Bent."

"Okay, Bent," Parker said. "Don't kill Adams until I say so. Is that clear enough? That is, unless you want to do it for free?"

"I'd do it for free," Bent said, "but I'd sure rather get paid, so yeah, that's clear."

"Good," Parker said. "Since I pay the freight, I get to call the shots."

Bent shrugged and said, "That suits me. Say, you think I can get another one of these?"

Parker looked and saw that Bent was only half finished with his steak, but he waved at the waiter and mimed for him to bring another one anyway.

"And some more beer," Bent said.

Parker pointed to his own beer and then held up three fingers. The waiter understood.

"So maybe you should tell me what you do want me to do," Bent said. "That is, until Clint Adams does become the job."

TEN

Clint and Ike finished their meal, had pie to top it off. While they were waiting for the pie, Clint passed a wad of cash to Ike under the table. Ike pocketed it without trying to count it.

"Where do we meet these fellas with the poles?" Clint asked.

"We go back to the docks," Ike said. "There's a saloon tent there where they do their drinkin'. They also fight there, pretty much every night."

"Then we better get to them before they get drunk," Clint suggested.

"Drunk or sober, they'll be there in the mornin' once we pay 'em."

"You're going to pay them first?"

Ike shrugged. "It's the only way they'll take the job. They don't wanna head upriver, run into trouble, and then not get paid."

"And we don't want them to head upriver, dump

the equipment in the water, and then say they had trouble."

"If they do that, they don't get no other work," Ike said. "Naw, these guys'll do the job."

"I hope you're right."

"About this, I am."

Bent Miller, Hector, and Parker finished their meals—Bent eating two steaks in the time it took the others to eat one—and then also had some pie, and coffee.

"So what do I do tonight?" Bent asked.

"Keep an eye on Adams," Parker said. "I want to know what he does tonight."

"Okay."

"Then meet me at the Skagway Hotel in the morning, in the lobby," Miller said. "We're going to be heading upriver, and you're coming with us."

Bent touched his pocket, where Calvin Parker's five hundred dollars resided, and said, "You're payin' the freight."

"Hector says you have men. Partners?"

"I have some men who work for me," Bent said, "but if you want them, too, you gotta pay extra."

"Paying is not a problem for me," Parker said. "Ever!"

"Come on," Clint said, "let's get out of here before those three stand up."

"You worried about them?" Ike asked.

"That fella Bent's been looking over at me," Clint said. "Seems they told him who I was, so he might be getting some ideas."

"Okay, sure."

They stood up and headed for the door, but it would have been obvious if they skirted the table Parker, Hector, and Bent were sitting at, so they had to walk right past it.

"Mr. Adams!" Parker called.

Clint stopped short, Ike running into him from behind.

"Mr. Parker."

"If I'd thought of it earlier, you and your friend could have joined us."

Clint smiled and said, "I have the feeling we were all doing our own business."

"You're probably right," Parker said. "Do you know my associate, Bent Miller?"

"Can't say I do."

"Adams," Bent said, nodding.

"Miller. This is my partner, Ike Daly."

"Mr. Daly," Parker said, "a pleasure."

"Same here," Ike said.

"Perhaps we can have that drink while we're all still in Skagway," Parker said.

"Maybe," Adams said. "We'll have to see."

"Good night, then."

"Night," Clint said. He and Ike left the River.

Bent Miller watched Clint Adams walk out, then turned to Parker.

"He's worried about me."

"Is he?"

"I can tell."

"That's fine, then," Parker said. "That can work in our favor."

"Well," Bent said, "thanks for the meal, and the job."

"And the five hundred," Hector said. "Don't forget the five hundred."

Bent patted himself on the pocket where the money was and said, "I never forget the money."

The three men stood up and left the place.

"You were right," Ike said.

"About what?"

"Bent Miller," Ike said. "He's got his eyes on you."

"Yeah. I'm going to have to deal with him at some point."

"Maybe we can get out of Skagway without seeing him again."

"Let's hope so," Clint said, "for his sake."

Parker, Hector, and Bent stepped outside, didn't see Clint Adams or Ike Daly anywhere.

"Sure got away from here quick, didn't they?" Bent asked.

"They probably had business to conduct elsewhere," Parker said. "Hector, I believe you do, too."

"Yes, sir."

"Maybe you should take Bent with you," Parker suggested.

"I'm supposed to meet my men, but we can do that," Bent said. "No problem." He slapped Hector on the back, causing the man to jump. "I'll take care of your boy."

ELEVEN

Ike took Clint down to the docks, where they found the tent saloon called the Gold Mine.

"That's optimistic," Clint said.

"Huh?"

"I guess the owners were hoping this would be their gold mine."

"I bet it is," Ike said. "They do a helluva business here."

They entered and Clint saw what his friend meant. Almost everybody there was shoulder to shoulder, and it was noisy as hell with conversation. And—true to what Ike had told him—there were a couple of fights going on. From what Clint could see, though, it was mostly harmless wrestling by drunks who couldn't hurt each other.

"Make way, make way," Ike said, elbowing his way to the bar. Men moved for him without giving him a second look. "Beer?" he asked Clint.

Clint nodded.

"Two beers!" Ike shouted.

Clint wondered how long that would take, but a bartender appeared almost immediately with two mugs. He couldn't see much behind the bar, but there must have been more than one barman.

Ike handed Clint a beer, then stepped away from the bar. The space he'd made quickly sealed itself.

"See your boys here?" Clint asked.

"Not yet," Ike said. "Maybe they're in the back."

"Take a look," Clint said. "I'll wait here, instead of both of us trying to fight our way through the crowd."

"Okay."

Ike took his beer and worked his way through the crowd. Clint marveled at how his friend was able to do this without spilling a drop, but then he was swallowed up by the crowd.

There were a couple of arguments going on at the bar that could become fights pretty soon. Clint vowed to keep out of either one, so he moved farther away from the bar. In doing so, somebody bumped into him, spilling some of his beer.

"Sorry, sweetie," a girl said.

He looked down at her. She was wearing Levi's and a plaid shirt, but was carrying a tray of drinks.

"You're a saloon girl?" he asked.

"That's right," the pretty brunette said. "Too damn cold up here for dresses. Let me get you another beer, since I spilled that one."

"Still plenty of it left."

"Just stay here, sweetie," she said. "I'll be right back."

He decided not to fight it. A free beer was a free beer.

While he waited, he finished what was left of the first one. As he thought, one of the arguments at the bar turned into another wrestling match. Seemed like it was also too cold to throw punches.

"Here ya go, hon," the girl said. She held out a full mug, and when Clint took it, she snatched the almost empty one from his hand. "You've got to watch where you're goin' in here."

"You bumped into me," he reminded her.

"No, I didn't."

"You apologized." He held up his fresh beer to indicate her mode of apology.

She smiled and said, "I was bein' nice."

She flounced away to serve the rest of her drinks. Clint thought her round butt was more interesting in the trousers than it would have been in a dress.

He looked around at that moment, saw Ike come out from the crowd with half of his beer intact. He'd either drunk the half, or spilled it.

"You find them?" Clint asked.

"Yeah, they're in the back. They said they'd meet us outside."

"When?"

"In a few minutes."

Clint looked around for the girl, but there was no sign of her.

"You got another beer?" Ike asked.

"Yeah, a free one."

"How come?"

"I'll tell you later. Drink up, and we'll go outside and wait for your friends."

"Suits me."

They finished their beers, and Ike elbowed his way back to the bar to set the empties down, then they went out the door.

Outside the wrestling matches had finished and there was enough space to stretch.

"It's colder out here," Clint said, "but at least there's room to breathe."

"You'll get used to the cold."

"I hope so."

"We'll get you some good long johns."

Clint nodded. Long johns would help a lot.

They waited about fifteen minutes and no one appeared from the saloon.

"Are they coming?" Clint asked. "I thought you said these fellas were reliable."

"They are," Ike said. "They'll be here. Let's just give them a little more time."

Clint nodded, and settled down to wait.

TWELVE

Parker and Hector made their way back to their hotel while Bent Miller followed Clint Adams and his friend Ike to the Gold Mine Saloon. Bent remained outside when they went in, and was still there when they came out. It looked as if they were waiting for someone.

He decided to try a little experiment.

A couple of blocks away he found five men looking for trouble. They did not, however, want it from Bent Miller.

"We ain't lookin' for you, Bent," one of them said.

"That's okay, Rango," Bent said. "I just got a tip for you about some fellas who are carryin' a lot of money."

Four of the men perked up, but Rango asked, "How much is a lot?"

"More than the five of you have got on you now," Bent said.

"Okay," Rango said. "That's a lot." He turned and looked at his friends, who all nodded.

"Okay," Rango said, "so where are these fellas?"

Bent told them . . .

Clint saw the men well in advance of Ike. Ike saw that Clint's attention had been drawn, so he turned and looked.

"Uh-oh," he said.

"You armed?" Clint asked.

"I got a gun in my coat."

"Make it available, Ike. In case you have to reach for it."

Ike opened his coat.

The five men approached, fanned out. Clint's gun and holster were clear of his jacket.

"How are you fellas doin'?" one of them asked.

"We're doing fine," Clint said.

"That's what we hear," the man said. "We hear you're doin' real good. Like you got some money you'd like to donate to us so we can be doin' fine, too."

"No," Clint said.

"No? Whataya mean, no?"

"No money for you," Clint said. "Move along."

"Move along?" the man asked incredulously. He looked around at his friends, who flanked him.

"'Move along,' he says. 'No money,' he says."

The other men laughed. They were all wearing guns, but Clint noticed that two of them had their jacket hems over the butts of their pistols. No need to worry about them unless they made a point of freeing them.

"Okay," the middle man said, "hand over the money."

"What money?" Ike asked. "We don't have any money."

"We wuz told different."

"Really?" Clint asked. "By who?"

"That don't matter."

Clint looked around them, beyond them, into the shadows. He thought he saw someone watching. He thought he knew who it was. Somebody who was interested in standing back and watching, seeing what he had left.

These men were a sacrifice.

"You don't want to do this," he said to them.

"Why not?" the middle man, Rango, asked.

"Because we might be carrying money," Clint said, "but it's not enough for all of you to die for."

"Hey," one of the other men said, "who is this guy? He thinks he can kill five of us?"

"He knows he can," Ike said.

The men looked at him.

"Whataya mean, he knows he can?" Rango asked. "How can he know that?"

"Because," Ike said, "his name is Clint Adams."

All five men stared at Clint.

"You know," Ike continued, "the Gunsmith?"

THIRTEEN

Clint had spent many years trying not to use that name, but these days if using it could help avoid killing, he used it.

"That's right," he said. "Still want my money?"

The five men exchanged glances, but it was the middle man who made the decision for all of them by going for his gun.

Clint drew, fired once, killed Rango.

The other four men froze.

Ike took out this gun, but Clint put out a hand to stay his action.

"You men still want our money?" he asked the four.

The four men remained frozen.

"Come on," Clint said, "one of you has to speak for you all, or you all die."

"No, no," one of them said. "No, we don't want nothin'."

"Then like I said before, move along."

They didn't have to be told again. They scattered and ran in four different directions.

Across the street in the shadows, Bent Miller smiled, almost laughed. The name had saved Clint Adams. Oh, he'd been fast when he drew, but he'd only had to shoot one man. Had the others had the nerve to draw, the Gunsmith would be dead.

In fact, from where he stood, Bent Miller could have drawn and killed the Gunsmith now, but then he wouldn't get paid for it.

He remained where he was, not wanting Adams to see him. Not yet anyway.

"What was that about?" Ike asked, putting his gun away.

Clint's eyes still scanned the shadows as he ejected the spent shell, replaced it, and holstered his gun.

"Somebody was testing me," he said.

"Did you pass?"

"Maybe."

From behind them four men came out of the saloon.

"Ike?" one of them said.

Clint turned quickly, but Ike said, "Easy. We're waitin' for them."

"Well, okay, then," Clint said. "You take care of business, and I'll keep watch."

Ike turned and approached the four men who had come out of the Gold Mine. Clint continued to study the shadows.

* * *

Bent Miller knew that Clint Adams felt his presence. Should he step out, get it over with right now?

The smaller man, Ike, did his business with the other men while Adams kept scanning the shadows with his eyes. He couldn't see Bent, but he could feel him.

One of the things Bent Miller prided himself on was his patience. He could stand still, right where he was, until he took root if he had to. He had no doubt he could outlast the Gunsmith.

No doubt.

Clint could hear the rustle of cash as money changed hands, and then the men dispersed. Ike appeared at his side again.

"See anybody?"

"No," Clint said, "but he's there."

"Who?"

"Bent Miller."

"You think he sent those men?"

"He told them we were holding a lot of money," Clint said. "That's all they had to hear."

"And he stood back to watch them kill us."

"He wanted to see me in action."

"And he did."

"Not the way he wanted, though," Clint said. He looked at Ike. "You talked them out of it."

"I did?"

"You told them who I am."

"Oh, that," Ike said.

"All right," Clint said. "Is our business done?"

"Yeah, I paid them. In the morning our boats will start upriver."

"And when do we start upriver?"

"Soon after that," Ike said.

"Then we can go back to the hotel now and get some rest?"

"You don't wanna go back into the saloon for another beer?"

Clint thought a moment about the girl who had brought him the free beer, and then said, "Oh hell, why not?"

FOURTEEN

Only after Clint Adams and Ike Daly went back into the saloon did Bent Miller come out from the shadows. The body of the dead man remained lying in the street.

There was no formal law in Skagway at that time, so the body would probably stay there until someone decided to move it. Nobody would be looking for whoever killed him. His four partners would probably never be seen again, so the only men in town who knew that Clint Adams killed Rango were Ike Daly and Bent Miller.

Not that it mattered. Skagway was what Tombstone, and Dodge, and Abilene used to be in the old days—lawless.

Bent left the area, leaving behind him the lights and noise of the Gold Mine Saloon. There were other saloons where he could get a drink, and a woman, and he wanted both.

                              *   *   *

Clint came back to the entrance of the saloon and
watched as Bent Miller came out from the shadows. He
sipped his beer, then turned when someone tapped him
on the shoulder.

"Were you lookin' for me?" the girl asked.

The girl's name was Lana, and somehow she managed
to have a tent of her own.

As they entered, Clint saw he would not be able to
stand up straight, the tent was so small.

"Don't worry," Lana said, opening the front of the
stove and lighting it. "You won't be standing up for long."

The stove gave off immediate heat. Lana's bed was
a cot that would not support both their weights.

"Sit," she said, "while I make a bed on the floor."

Clint sat on the cot.

"I should have said," he told her, "I don't, uh, pay—"

"I'm not askin' for money," she said. "I just want your
cock in me."

He was shocked, although he tried not to show it.

"Too bold?" she asked, spreading blankets on the floor.

"If it doesn't bother you, it doesn't bother me," he
said. "But why me?"

"Because in the mornin' you'll be gone," she said.
"A lot of these fellas will be here tomorrow, and the next
day, and the next day. I don't need a lovesick man fol-
lowin' me around for days."

"But there are others who won't be here."

She smiled, knelt in front of him, and touched his face.

"You appealed to me," she said. "Isn't that enough?
And it helps that you've had a bath."

She stared into his eyes while her fingers undid the buttons of her own shirt. When she removed it, she shivered for just a second, and the nipples of her small, firm breasts stiffened. Next, she worked on the buttons of his shirt. When she removed it, she ran her hands over his chest. They were warm, but he also shivered.

He leaned down and kissed her. In the midst of the kiss, she pulled him down to the blankets. She undid his gun belt, which he laid on the cot right next to them, and then his trousers. She reached inside, grasped his penis, and said, "Ahhh."

He closed his eyes as she stroked him, then grasped his trousers and pulled them all the way down. She kissed his belly, his sides, his hips, and his thighs, finally centering on his hard cock. She held it in her hands, kissed the underside, licked it, wet it, made him moan before she took it fully into her mouth . . .

It was nickel night at the whorehouse. Men came in with their pockets jangling, but Bent Miller knew they were idiots. For most of them, one nickel would do the trick, and then they would be done for the evening.

But not him. He had been there many times before, and the girls knew that he would use three or four of them before he was done. Estralita said he was "much man," and Delores said he was "insatiable," although most of the other girls didn't know what that meant.

The madam, Lily, met him at the door with a big smile and a powdered bosom that threatened to spill out of her dress. Bent hoped it wouldn't, because he was afraid her tits would fall right to the floor.

"I knew you'd be here on nickel night, Bent," she said.

"Wouldn't miss it."

"I've got a new girl, just came in on the boat today. Ain't been touched yet."

"I ain't interested in no virgin, Lily."

"No, not a virgin," she said. "I just mean she ain't been touched by anybody since she got here this afternoon."

"Oh," Bent said, "well, that's okay, then. I might as well start with her."

"Out back, tent number three."

Bent looked at the girls who were seated on pillows in the main tent. Blonds, brunettes, and redheads, black girls and Chinese girls. Lily offered them all to the men of Skagway.

"What's her name?" he asked.

"Francesca," she said, "but you can call her Frankie."

"What's she look like?"

"White skin, black hair, nice body. You'll like her."

"Okay," he said, "but save me the Chinee and the black one."

"Okay, Bent."

Bent liked to sample women of all sizes and color. He knew lots of men who said one pussy was like another, but they all felt and tasted different to him.

"Tent three?" he said.

"That's right," Lily said. "Just go in. I been savin' her for you. She's waitin'."

Bent walked through the tent and went out the back flap. There he saw smaller tents in a row. He counted, and went into number three.

FIFTEEN

Clint rolled Lana onto her back, pulled her trousers down, and discarded them. Her skin was white and smooth. She'd had a bath earlier in the day, but she still smelled like she'd been at work—smoke and sweat, not an unpleasant combination of odors, especially since the sweat was her own.

He kissed her legs and thighs, worked his lips over her belly to her breasts. He held them, squeezed them, bit the nipples. Her kissed her neck, her shoulders, even her armpits, where the dark hair tickled his nose.

"I stink," she said, trying to pull his head away.

"Girl sweat never stinks," he told her, licking her there.

"Omigod!" she said. "You're getting me so excited."

He crossed to her other armpit, kissed her, then worked his way down her body. Now he pressed his face to the dark bush of hair, probed into it with his tongue until he found her sticky wet and ready. He licked her until she screamed, then mounted her and dove into her.

Most women's pussies were hot, but in Alaska it felt like he was driving himself into molten lava.

"Ohhh, God," she moaned as he fucked her. "Yes, this is what I wanted."

The interior of the tent was warm from the stove, and from the heat given off by their bodies, which had both begun to sweat. In a little while they'd be cold as their bodies cooled, but at that moment it didn't matter if they were in Alaska, or down South in New Orleans. They were both hot . . .

Bent Miller entered the tent. The woman sitting on the cot looked up at him quickly, with wide eyes—not exactly frightened eyes, but surprised.

"Are you Frankie?" he asked.

"That's right."

"So this is tent three."

"Y-Yes."

She was wearing a robe, but he could see that what Lily had told him was true. She sure had black hair, and her skin was very white, indeed.

"I'm Bent Miller. Did Lily tell you I'd be here?"

"Yes, she did."

It was warm inside, thanks to a small stove in the corner.

"Stand up," he told her.

She did.

"Take off that robe."

She removed the robe and he liked what he saw. A bush of black hair between her slender thighs, tits like peaches. He took them in his hands, palmed them, popped the nipples with his big thumbs.

"We're gonna have some fun," he told her.

She nodded, winced when he squeezed her nipples between his thumbs and forefingers.

"Just stand there," he said. "I'm gonna get undressed."

"A-All right."

He removed his hat and his shirt, then undid his gun belt and set it aside, where he could still get to it if he had to. He removed his boots and trousers, until all he had on was his long johns. He was going to take his time taking them off, because he liked how impressed the girls looked when they saw how big he was down there.

But before he did that, he reached for her, ran his hands over her body some more. He turned her around so he could paw her ass, slap her ass cheeks until they were red.

"You're a little skinny, but nice and firm," he told her.

"Um, thank you."

He run his thumb down the crease between her ass cheeks, found her anus with it, stroked that a bit, then put his thumb in his mouth, wetting it. He went back to her anus and pressed his thumb to it, then slid it into her butt hole.

She jumped, startled.

"You ever had it in your ass?" he asked.

"N-No," she said.

He slid his thumb in and out of her ass and said, "Then you're in for somethin' new."

He took his thumb from her butt hole, stuck his fingers into the waist band of his long johns, and peeled them down. By now because he had played with her body some, his cock was fully hard. It sprang out from his underwear and her eyes widened.

"Ain't seen that before, have you?" he asked her, stepping out of his long johns and leaving them on the floor.

"N-No," she said. "Never."

"Well, then," he told her, "come on over here and get acquainted, girl!"

She got down on her knees . . .

SIXTEEN

Clint and Lana lay huddled together beneath blankets. Although the stove still gave off heat, the fact that they were covered with sweat by the time they concluded their coupling led them both to be chilled.

"So when exactly would you be leavin'?" she asked him.

"In the morning."

"Too bad."

"I thought that was the whole point," he said. "That I would be leaving."

"Well," she said, "that was before you did what you did to me. I guess I wouldn't mind if you stay around a few days."

"I can't do that."

"Or," she said, "passed this way again?"

"Maybe, when it's time for me to leave Alaska," he said.

"Well," she said, snuggling closer, "that will give me somethin' to look forward to."

She slid her hand down to his crotch.

"The night's not over yet," he pointed out.

She closed her hand over him and said, "I can see that," with delight. "Not ready to go to sleep?"

"Oh no," he said, "being with a beautiful woman has a way of keeping me awake."

"So unlike other men," she said in his ear, "in so many ways."

Bent Miller left Frankie lying on the floor, curled up into a ball. The pain he'd caused her had rendered her unconscious. Too bad, he thought. She had been pretty good. When she woke, she wouldn't be much good to Madam Lily for a few days.

He left her tent, went back to the main tent to claim his other two girls, the black and the Chinee . . .

Ike awoke in the middle of the night as Clint slipped back into the room.

"Didn't think you'd be back," Ike muttered.

"I need to get some sleep," Clint said. "After all, we're starting a long journey tomorrow."

"Yeah, we are," Ike said, "but not until after we get some breakfast."

Clint undressed and fell onto his bed. By that time Ike was back to snoring.

SEVENTEEN

Ike awoke first, and his moving about the room woke up Clint. Daybreak was streaming through the window.

"It's cold," Clint said.

"You think it's cold now?" Ike asked. "Wait 'til we get to Forty Mile. Come on, I'm hungry."

To his surprise, so was Clint. He didn't think he'd be ready to rise so early, but his insistent stomach took precedence.

He stood up and caught something Ike tossed him from across the room.

"Long johns," he said.

"I picked them up yesterday," Ike said.

"Thanks," Clint said. "These will help a lot."

He washed in the basin. Dried himself quickly, but not before he got even colder. It was only when he pulled on the long johns that he got relief. He dressed over them, and was surprised at how much better he felt. He strapped on his gun and turned to his friend.

"Breakfast," he said.

Ike led Clint to a small café in a tent, where he said it was usually too expensive for him to eat.

"But everybody says they got the best breakfast."

They were seated and served, and Clint saw that his friend was right. The steak and eggs were prepared perfectly, and the coffee was hot and strong.

"There are a lot of good cooks in Alaska," he said. "I hope some of them have found their way to Forty Mile."

"Don't worry," Ike said. "Some of them are there."

"Good."

"After this we can go to the docks and make sure our boats got on their way earlier."

"You said the men you hired are reliable."

"They are," Ike said. "I just want to make sure nothin' went wrong."

"Okay," Clint said.

"And we can check on our boat. It should be ready and waiting."

"And our supplies?"

"Should be on board."

"I hope you're right, and that there's enough gold at Forty Mile to make all these preparations worth it."

"Don't worry," Ike said. "There is."

They finished their breakfast and Clint paid the bill. As they walked out the front flap, Clint looked around, wondering if they were being watched.

"Anythin'?" Ike asked.

"No," Clint said.

"He was out there last night, though?"

"Yep. I saw him leave."

"If he's gonna try somethin', it'll have to be soon, or we'll be gone."

"Suits me."

On the way to the docks they passed the Gold Mine Saloon. The body was gone from out front.

"They really need some law here," Ike said.

"Maybe somebody should just appoint himself sheriff," Clint suggested.

"Like you?"

"No, not me."

"No, I meant somebody like you, who can handle a gun," Ike said. "It would have to be somebody like that."

"Sure."

At the docks, Clint waited while Ike checked with the dockmaster to make sure their boats left on time. He scanned the area, and was sure that neither Bent Miller nor anyone else was watching them. Miller must have learned what he needed to learn the night before.

Ike returned and said, "The boats got off on time, very early."

"Good."

"And our boat is being loaded right now," Ike said. "Our men are taking care of it."

"Then I guess we better go back to the hotel and pack."

"Shoulda done that this mornin'," Ike said.

"That's okay," Clint said. "I want to say good-bye to someone first anyway."

"Maybe shoulda done that last night," Ike said.

"You're probably right," Clint said, "but I didn't, so . . ."

They headed back to the hotel. When they got there, they found three men waiting for them in the lobby.

"Clint Adams?" one man asked. He was heavyset, in his forties, with a busy mustache. He was wearing a dark suit, a white shirt, and a derby hat. The other men were younger, but dressed the same.

"What can I do for you?"

"My name is Sean Casey, Mr. Adams," the man said. Then he pulled aside his coat to show Clint a badge on his chest. "Federal marshal."

"I thought there was no law in Skagway," Clint said.

"Well," Casey said, "actually, law has come to Skagway, Mr. Adams . . . and it's meself."

EIGHTEEN

Calvin Parker refused to eat in a café or restaurant that was in a tent, so he and Hector went back to where they'd had dinner the night before. They found Bent Miller waiting for them in front.

"Good morning, Mr. Miller."

"Mr. Parker. I assumed I was invited to breakfast?"

"Sure, why not?" Parker said. "Come on in."

They entered and took a table.

Over coffee, Parker asked, "Did you see what Clint Adams was up to last night?"

"I did," Miller said. "He killed a man."

"What?"

"He got into a dispute last night and solved it with his gun."

"Where did this happen?"

"In front of the Gold Mine Saloon."

"Did he also have a run-in with the law?" Hector asked.

"There is no law in Skagway," Bent said.

"You're mistaken," Hector said. "We came over on the boat with the new law in Skagway."

"What?"

"Three men, but one of them was a federal marshal," Hector said. "An Irishman named Sean Casey."

"I didn't know they were bringin' law into Skagway," Bent said.

"Well, now that they're here," Parker said, "could it be possible Clint Adams will end up in a cell?"

"Since I'm pretty sure they haven't had time to build a jail, I'd say no," Bent said, "but if this Casey fella is determined to be the law here, I'd say he's probably talkin' to Adams right now."

"And maybe it would help him to have a witness who saw the entire altercation," Parker said.

"Uh, I don't think I'd make a real good witness for the law," Bent said.

"Maybe," Parker said, "we should let the new marshal be the judge of that."

"I wouldn't even know where to find the man," Bent said.

Parker smiled and said, "We'll figure it out."

Clint was surprised to learn not only that Sean Casey was a federal marshal, but that he had come to Skagway on the same ship.

"I never saw you on the ship," he said.

"No one was supposed to see me, sir," Marshal Casey said. "Can we talk somewhere?"

They were still standing in the lobby of the Skagway Hotel.

"What's wrong with right here?" Clint said. "We were on our way up to our room to pick up our things."

"Leaving Skagway, are you?"

"As soon as we can," Clint said.

"Well, not so quickly, I'm afraid."

"And why not?"

Casey smiled and said, "That's what we must talk about."

"Do you need my friend?"

"Who is he?"

"Ike Daly."

Casey didn't even look at Ike.

"I have no business with anyone by that name."

"Ike, why don't you go up and pack your things," Clint suggested. "I'll be along . . . as soon as I can."

"Okay, Clint." Ike looked worried, but he went up the stairs, leaving Clint with Marshal Casey.

"Why don't we step outside?" the marshal suggested.

"It's cold out there."

"Really? I find the bracing weather here invigorating."

The other two men with him flanked Clint.

"These your deputies?"

"They are my . . . colleagues, and they would also like you to step outside."

"I think I'd like a better look at your badge."

"Certainly."

The marshal pulled his coat aside. If the badge was a phony, it was a damned good one.

"Satisfied?" Casey asked.

"Sure," Clint said. "Let's step outside."

The four men stepped to the door and outside.

"What's this about, Marshal?"

"Well, we know what this is about, don't we, Mr. Adams? You killed a man last night."

"In self-defense."

"Do you have a witness?"

"Yes," Clint said, "we just sent him away. You said you had no business with him."

"Well, perhaps I was wrong," the marshal said. "I'll certainly speak with him, but do you have any witnesses who aren't friends of yours? Someone who could be . . . dispassionate?"

"Dispassionate?" Clint said. "No, I have no one who would be dispassionate. Ike's my only witness, and his life was in danger, too."

"I see."

"There were four or five men, Marshal, who tried to rob us. I only killed one. The rest got the message and abandoned the idea."

"I see. I must tell you, Mr. Adams, if I had an office and a jail cell, I'd be inclined to keep you there while I look into this."

"It's just as well you don't have a jail, Marshal," Clint retorted, "because I'd be inclined to resist."

The other two men stiffened, still flanking Clint.

"You should probably tell your colleagues to relax, Marshal . . . and while you're at it, have them move."

"Gents," Casey said, and the two men moved to either side of him.

"Where are you off to today, Mr. Adams?"

"I'm going upriver to Forty Mile."

"And you'll be there how long?"

"Indefinitely," Clint said. "If you decide to arrest me, you'll find me there. But I don't think that'll be the case."

"I suppose we'll have to wait and see," the marshal said.

"Are we done?"

"For now," Marshal Casey said. "But I'll be in touch."

"Fine," Clint said. "I'll look forward to it."

Clint went back into the hotel, and up to his room to pack.

"You really gonna let him go, Marshal?" one of the other men asked.

Casey looked at the man and couldn't recall his name.

"Would you like to try to take him into custody?" he asked.

"Not me," the man said.

Casey looked at the other man. "You?"

"No, sir!"

"Then we'll let him go upriver," Casey said. "I'll know where to find him."

NINETEEN

As Clint entered the room, Ike looked up from the bed and asked, "What the hell was that about?"

"Apparently we now have law in Alaska."

"In Skagway," Ike said. "We goin' to Forty Mile."

"I figure the marshal wouldn't be shy about coming to Forty Mile if he had to."

"And this was about last night?"

"That's right."

"That was self-defense."

"That's what I told him."

"Did he believe you?"

"I don't know," Clint said. "I think he's going to go looking for witnesses."

"Think he'll find any?"

Clint shrugged. "Somebody could have been watching from the saloon. But my guess is he'll be waiting downstairs for you when we get there."

"What should I tell him?"

"Just tell him the truth, Ike. Just tell him what happened."

"I can do that."

Clint packed his bag and grabbed his rifle.

"Okay, let's go down and get this over with."

As he predicted, they found the marshal and his "colleagues" waiting in the lobby.

"Mr. Daly," the marshal said, "a moment of your time?"

"Sure," Ike said.

"I'll wait outside," Clint said.

He stepped out in front of the hotel to wait. As he stood there, he saw a man in a red uniform walking toward him. It looked like a military uniform. His black boots were polished to a high sheen.

"Excuse me," the man said, "can you tell me if this is the hotel where Clint Adams is staying?"

"I'm Clint Adams," Clint said. "Can I help you?"

"Sir, I'm Trooper Allan Craig of the Northwest Canadian Mounted Police. I understand you were forced to kill a man yesterday."

"The Canadian Police?"

"Yessir," Craig said. "Due to the proximity of Skagway to the Yukon, my superiors felt a need to establish a presence here."

"And you're it?"

"Um, yessir, I am it."

"You do know that there's a U.S. federal marshal in town also?"

"Yessir, we're aware that the U.S. has felt the need

to send someone, as well. I don't see any reason why we can't coexist."

"Well," Clint said, "you might want to go into the lobby and let him know that."

"Is he here? I see he's ahead of me."

"Yes."

"Has he interviewed you?"

"Yes."

"Could I ask you to repeat to me what you told him?"

"Sure, why not. I shot a man in self-defense when he and his friends tried to rob us. The other men then ran away."

"You let them go?"

"I did."

"You didn't feel the need to make a citizen's arrest?" the trooper asked.

"I did not."

"Or turn them in?"

"To who?" Clint said. "Last night I was under the impression there was no law in Skagway. I now know there are two lawmen here from two different countries. But there's still not a jail, right?"

"Right."

"Well, your colleague, Marshal Casey, is in the lobby talking to my friend Ike, who was the only witness."

"Very good. Thank you." The trooper started into the lobby, then stopped. "Are you leaving town?"

"That's why I'm holding my rifle and bag."

"Where are you going?"

"Upriver to a town called Forty Mile."

"I know it," the trooper said. "If I need anything else, I'll find you there."

"I understand it's pretty remote."

Trooper Craig smiled.

"I'm Canadian," he said. "I'm used to places that are remote. Thank you."

The trooper went into the lobby. Clint waited another fifteen minutes, and then Ike came out.

"Finished?" Clint asked.

"I think so. Neither of them lawmen was talkin' to me anymore. They was arguin' when I left."

"Let them argue," Clint said. "We've got a boat to catch."

TWENTY

Calvin Parker opened the door of his room in response to a knock. Hector was standing in the lobby.

"Everything all right?" Parker asked.

"I've got some information."

"Come in, then."

Hector came in and closed the door.

"This place is a dump," Parker said. "Are you sure this was the best place in Skagway?"

"Best place in Alaska," Hector said. "It's not going to get much better in Forty Mile."

"Yes," Parker said, "we'll talk about that. Right now let's hear what you have to say."

"We thought there was no law up here," Hector said. "We were wrong."

"How wrong?"

"Twice as wrong as we could've been."

"And what's that mean?"

"There's a U.S. marshal and a Canadian lawman in town."

"Canadian?"

"Royal Mounted Police."

Parker rubbed his jaw and walked around the room. When he got to the window, he looked down at the muddy street. Then he turned and looked at Hector.

"They're going to be fighting for jurisdiction," he said. "That will probably keep them busy."

"Maybe."

"What have they been doing?"

"They both talked to Clint Adams about the man he killed."

"Did Miller talk to them?"

"No."

"Good. Tell him to forget it. He doesn't need to be a witness."

"Okay," Hector said.

"Here's the other thing," Parker said. "Hire Bent Miller to go to Forty Mile with you."

"With me?"

"That's right."

"You're not going?"

"Like you said," Parker replied, "it won't get any better up there, and I can hardly stand it here."

"Are you going back?"

"No," Parker said, "I don't want to be that far away from my mine."

"So what are you going to do?"

"I'm going to stay here and have a house built for myself," Parker said. "Someplace a man like me deserves to live. And I might have a hotel built—a good hotel."

"All that?"

"Don't worry," Parker said, "It'll be months before you get back here. It will all be done by then."

"Miller will be reporting to me?"

"Yes," Parker said. "Make him understand that."

"Me? Make him understand?"

"You're my right hand, Hector," Parker said. "Start acting like it. Make Bent Miller respect you."

"How do I do that?"

"Figure it out," Parker said. "You're going to be in charge in Forty Mile, Hector. It'll be easier if you have Bent Miller as your right-hand man. Understand?"

"I do."

"All right, then," Parker said. "When do the boats leave?"

"A couple of hours."

"Then you better get on it," Parker said.

TWENTY-ONE

Clint and Ike got to the docks. There were four men waiting for them on a flat boat. They were all holding poles. On the boat were enough supplies for the ride upriver, which would take weeks.

Ike made the introductions.

"This is Clint Adams, my partner," he said. "He's also the moneyman, so if the boat starts to sink, he's the one you should save. Clint, these are Ben, Phil, Dallas, and Jud."

"Boys," Clint said, nodding. He wished Ike hadn't said what he did about him being the moneyman. He might be the one they saved if the boat sank, but he'd also be the one they killed if they decided to rob them.

They all nodded.

"These boys have been up and down these rivers a million times," Ike said. "They're the best."

"Then we might as well get going, before one of those lawmen decides to keep us here."

"Boys," Ike said, "all aboard."

Hector found Bent Miller in one of the saloon tents, sitting alone over a beer. There was a lot of activity going on around him, but the man didn't seem to notice.

Hector got himself a beer and carried it to Miller's table.

"Mind if I join you?"

Bent looked up at him.

"We got some business?"

"We might, if I can sit and talk to you."

"Go ahead," Bent said, kicking the chair out for Hector to sit in.

"I'm heading upriver to Forty Mile today," Hector said.

"And?"

"I want you to come with me."

"What for?"

"I want you to be my right-hand man."

"What about your boss, Parker?"

"He's not coming."

"So you'd be number one up there, and I'd be number two?"

"That's right."

"Will I get paid like a number two?"

"Absolutely."

"Will I have to make any mining decisions?"

"I'll take care of the mining operation," Hector said.

"And what do I take care of?"

Hector took a deep breath. This was where he had

to show some courage, try and establish the pecking order right from the beginning.

"Whatever I tell you to take of."

Bent stared at Hector for a while. Hector thought if he looked away, he'd be lost, so he continued to stare back at the gunman.

"Yeah, okay," Bent said finally, "and when I don't have anythin' to do?"

"Do what you want," Hector said. "Just be available at a moment's notice."

"I could do that," Bent said. "When do we leave?"

"In about two hours," Hector said. "We'll go up the Yukon till we get to Forty Mile River—"

"I know the way to Forty Mile," Bent said.

"Have you been there before?"

"Once."

"Okay, then," Hector said. "Meet me at the dock in two hours, and be packed."

"I'll be there," Bent said. "How about my boys?"

"How many?"

"Two of 'em."

"Can you pay them out of your pay?"

Bent thought, then said, "If I'm really gettin' paid like a number two, yeah."

"Okay," Hector said, standing up. "Bring them."

"We'll be there . . . boss."

Satisfied, Hector left the saloon and went to the dock to be sure the boats would be ready.

As Clint and Ike boarded their boat, Clint noticed four similar boats farther down the docks, all loaded with equipment.

"Whataya think?" Ike asked, seeing where his friend was looking.

"Seems to be the only person with enough money for an outfit like that is Calvin Parker."

"Well," Ike said, "just because he's leavin' from here and goin' upriver don't mean he's goin' to Forty Mile."

"Any other strikes up there?"

Ike hesitated, then said, "Not that I heard."

"Then we may have some competition."

"My stake is already filed," Ike said.

"When's the last time you were in Forty Mile?" Clint asked.

"Two months ago, maybe more."

"A lot can happen in two months."

Ike looked at Clint.

"Somebody tries to jump my claim, Clint, I ain't gonna like it."

"Since we're partners, Ike," Clint said, "I'm not going to be too happy either. Especially after I came all this way."

"We better get movin', then," Ike said. "From the look of things, we'll beat them to Forty Mile easy."

Ike addressed the four pole men and said, "Let's get movin'!"

"Okay, boss," one of them said.

The men all dug their poles into the soft river bottom, each of them standing in a different corner. As they pushed off, the boat started to move slowly away from the dock.

Clint thought the trip was probably going to take six months at this rate—or six *years*—but once they cleared the dock and got out into the river, he was surprised at how quickly the boat moved. Apparently the four men were used to working together. They pushed in unison and gathered much more speed than Clint would have thought possible.

TWENTY-TWO

When Hector got to the dock, he saw Clint Adams and his partner Ike pushing off. From the lack of equipment on their boat, he assumed they had sent it ahead of them. That didn't concern him. There was no way their equipment could match what Calvin Parker's money had bought.

He walked along the dock until he reached their boats, and carefully boarded each boat to check the cargo. He lifted tarps to look underneath, and by the time he was done, he was satisfied that everything was there. Some of the equipment had been dropped while being unloaded from the ship, but they wouldn't know if it was damaged until they reached Forty Mile and put it to work. Supposedly, they had a man in place there who would be able to fix any damage. If they needed to bring in new equipment, that was going to set them back months, and they could not afford that.

That wasn't something he looked forward to telling Calvin Parker.

Parker drank his coffee and considered the man seated across from him.

"You're supposed to be the best carpenter in town," he said.

"I am," the burly man said.

"Then don't tell me you built the Skagway Hotel."

"Not me," he said. "They had their own men."

"Is there an architect in town?"

"I don't know what that is," the man said.

Parker wondered if he was making a mistake.

"He's the man who draws up the plans for a building," he said.

"Plans? Listen, mister, I build things. That means furniture, boats, houses, and I do it the best way I know how. I got men who work with me who are real good with hammer and nails. You want one of them archi—archy—whatever you said, you're gonna have to bring him in from south of here. That'll take time. How soon you want this house built?"

"As soon as possible," Parker said.

"You tell me what you want and when you want it, and you pay for it, and you'll get your house."

Parker gave it some thought. The man was right. It would take too long to bring in an architect and a builder from Seattle. And this man looked the part, and seemed confident enough.

"All right," he said, "you have the job."

The builder reached out and said, "I do things with a handshake, Mr. Parker."

Parker eyed the man's big, rough hand dubiously, but finally reached out and shook it.

Marshal Sean Casey stared down at the dead, brutalized whore.

"You know who did this?" Casey asked the madam, Lily.

"Sure do," she said. "Bent Miller."

"Miller."

The flap of the tent opened and a man stepped in. He wore a red uniform, a gun in a holster with a flap.

"What are you doin' here?" Casey asked.

"I heard a girl was murdered," Trooper Alan Craig said.

"There she is," Casey said, pointing to the girl on the floor.

Craig looked down and removed his hat. "Poor girl."

Casey, who had not removed his hat to this point, took it off now and said, "Yeah."

"You know who did it?" the trooper asked.

"I know," Lily said. "He's done this to girls before, but this is the first one he's ever killed."

"What was her name?" Craig asked.

"Frankie," Lily said. "Actually, Francesca. This was her first day."

"Too bad," Craig said.

"Ma'am, can you give us a minute?" Casey asked. The small tent was crowded with the three of them and the body in it.

She stepped out.

"The madam says Bent Miller did it," Casey told the trooper.

"Miller? Do you know him?"

"I know the name," Casey said. "And the man's reputation."

"Well then, let's go get him. We can't let him get away with this."

"Why do you keep sayin' 'we'?"

"Because we're the law," Craig said. "We may be from different countries, but we both still want the same thing—law and order."

Casey sighed and regarded the younger man. He put his hat back on.

"Bent Miller is on a boat going upriver," he said. "Left a little while ago."

"We have to go after him," Craig said. "Do you know where he went?"

"Forty Mile."

"I know where that is."

"Well, good. Then you can guide me."

"We'll have to get a boat."

"Can't we ride? I hate boats. I was sick the whole way here."

"It's a rough ride," Craig said. "Over snowy mountains and through snowbound passes."

"But you know the way?"

"Of course."

"Then we need to get two horses."

"Shouldn't one of us stay here in Skagway?"

"I have two deputies, I can leave them here. We have to show these people they can't get away with murder."

"All right," Trooper Craig said. "When do you want to leave?"

"Now," Casey said.

TWENTY-THREE

TWO MONTHS LATER . . .

Clint knocked mud off his boots before entering the tent he shared with Ike. It was something he was trying to get Ike to do, as well. Sharing a hotel room with him for one day in Skagway was nothing compared to the prospect of sharing a tent with him for months here in Forty Mile.

He ducked his head and entered the tent. They were camped just outside of the town of Forty Mile. Ike's claim was upriver. At the present time they were panning the riverbed with sluice boxes for gold, but the equipment was still being set up for them to do some serious mining. Once the sluice chutes were finished, they'd be able to get started.

Clint was about to pull his boots off with Ike appeared in the tent opening.

"They're here."

"Who's here?"

"The boats from that feller, Parker. We beat them by better'n a week."

"Are they unloading?"

"Right now," Ike said. "Whole lot of equipment."

"Do we know where they're setting up?"

"Not yet."

"That fellow Hector, is he here, too?"

"Yeah, he was on one of the boats with that other fella."

"Parker?"

"No, not the fella with the money," Ike said. "The other guy."

"Bent Miller?"

"That's him."

Clint stood up from his cot, strapped on his gun.

"What the hell would he be doing here, except looking for me?"

"Ya think?"

"I don't know what else, but maybe we should find out."

"How we gonna do that?"

Clint slapped his friend on the arm and said, "How about we just ask him?"

"You think he'll answer you?"

"We'll get some kind of answer," Clint said. "Come on."

Ike told Clint when they arrived in Forty Mile that he didn't recognize the place.

"There's buildings here," he said. "When I left, there was no buildings."

There was a trading post, a saloon, a livery, and a whorehouse. No hotel, which was why they were camped on the banks of the Forty Mile River, near their claim.

The trip upriver had been arduous and cold. Clint decided the first day to take a turn on the poles, and had one of the men show him the proper way to do it. He'd spell each of the men for a while, so they could all get some rest. After a few days Ike was shamed into doing the same thing. With the six of them working, they got up a good head of steam, and Ike said he'd never seen a boat go upriver so fast. Still, it took them almost two months to negotiate the better than fifteen hundred miles. By the time they arrived, they all had full beards, as after a few days on the boat they quit shaving. And washing, except for Clint, who would take a dip in the river every few days.

When they reached the town, Ike and Clint gave the four men their head for a few days, told them to come back after they'd blown off some steam and be ready to work.

Three of the men came back a few days later. They said the fourth man had been stabbed to death in a fight in the whorehouse over a girl. There was no law in Forty Mile, and there wouldn't be unless the U.S. marshal or the trooper made the trip upriver. There was no secret about who had killed Jud. A miner named Paul Ritten had stabbed him with his own knife.

"Gotta tell the truth," Ben said. "Jud started it, and Ritten finished it."

They put the three men to work with sluice boxes.

When Clint and Ike got to the river, the flat boats were still being offloaded. Both Hector and Bent Miller were supervising the work.

"Mr. Adams," Hector said. He and Miller were both

unshaven, and unwashed. Clint was surprised. He'd have thought Hector was the type to bathe every day.

"Hector," Clint said. "Nice to see you. Didn't know you were coming up to Forty Mile."

"Didn't know you'd be here," Hector said. "Quite a coincidence."

"Yes," Clint said, "a coincidence."

"Adams," Bent said, nodding.

"Miller."

"What's this place like?" Bent asked.

"Muddy," Clint said.

"Any women?"

"There's a whorehouse, a livery, a saloon, and a trading post for supplies."

"Any law?"

"None."

"Interesting."

"I thought you might find that interesting," Clint said. "What brings you up here?"

"Work."

"What kind?"

"Mr. Miller works for me," Hector said.

Bent smiled at Clint and said, "He's number one up here, I'm number two."

"What do you know about a mining operation?" Clint asked.

"Nothin'."

"That's my end," Hector said.

"And what's his end?" Clint asked.

"Whatever I tell him."

Clint studied Hector. The man had changed, by

necessity or design he didn't know, but it was clearly evident.

"Well," Clint said, looking at Bent, "that should make for an interesting job."

TWENTY-FOUR

Clint and Ike went to the saloon. The place still smelled like new wood—the walls, the floor, and the bar itself. Most of the inhabitants of Forty Mile were miners; therefore, this early in the day they were doing just that . . . mining.

But mining camps brought others, as well. There were gamblers, prostitutes, pickpockets, con men, and more.

The bartender greeted them as they approached the bar.

"How you two doin'?" he asked, setting them each up with beers.

"Fine," Ike said. "Thanks, Zeke."

"Heard a big outfit got to town today," Zeke said. "That true?"

"It's true a potentially big outfit got to town today," Clint said. "Whether they make it or not is another story."

"Guess we'll see," Zeke said. "'Scuse me." He went down the bar to serve another customer.

"So what are we gonna do?" Ike asked Clint.

"We're just gonna to keep going the way we have been," Clint said. "Keep panning until we're ready to do some digging."

"And what about this feller Hector, and Bent Miller?" Ike asked. "They work for that Parker feller. Hector's gonna run the mine, but what's Bent gonna do?"

"You heard Hector," Clint said. "Bent will do what he tells him to do."

"You know, if Bent kills you, I'm not gonna be able to go on."

"I'm touched."

"I won't have any money."

"Oh. Well, don't worry," Clint said. "He's not going to kill me."

"A man like Bent Miller? How's he gonna resist tryin' himself against the Gunsmith?"

"Maybe he'll try," Clint said, "but he won't succeed. Don't worry."

"How can you be so confident all the time?" Ike said. "Don't you expect to someday meet a faster gun?"

"I expect one day I'll meet the man who's going to kill me," Clint said. "I don't think he'll be faster."

"You mean a backshooter? A bushwhacker? Or the way Hickok went?"

"The way we all go," Clint said. "Hickok, Ben Thompson, Jesse James, Billy the Kid. There's too much history to think it won't happen—but I don't think Bent Miller is the man."

"Well, okay, then," Ike said. "I'm gonna get to the claim and do some work."

"I'll be along in a while to spell you," Clint said. He may have been the moneyman in their partnership, but he did what everyone else did on the boat—and he'd do his share of the mining work, as well.

Ike gulped down his beer and set the glass down.

"See ya later."

When he left, Clint still had half his beer. He sipped at it, looking around the mostly empty saloon tent. There were a couple of gamblers sitting at tables, waiting for some suckers. One of them was shuffling and reshuffling his cards; the other one was playing solitaire. They would sit and wait for miners to come in with some dust, or a few gold nuggets, and then relieve them of it. He had met them both. Jerry Masters was forty, had been gambling for a living for ten years. He was the shuffler. The other man, ten years older and gambling all his life, was Wes Handler. Clint had heard of Handler before, and was surprised to find the man in a mining camp in Alaska. He had not played poker with either one.

So, too, did the whores wait in their tents, hoping to get their hands on some of that gold before the gamblers got it.

There were a couple of saloon girls standing in a corner talking, waiting for customers to come in. Later, when the miners quit work and came to town, the girls would be busy delivering drinks and avoiding the grasping hands.

Clint waved to Zeke and said, "Two beers."

Zeke delivered them.

"You gonna drink with both hands?"

"One's for Handler," Clint said. "Thanks."

Clint picked up both beers and carried them to Wes Handler's table.

"Beer?" he asked.

Handler looked up at him and smiled. "Thanks. Wanna go head-to-head?"

"Not today," Clint said, setting the beer at Handler's elbow, "but I'll sit awhile and talk."

"By all means," Handler said.

Clint pulled out a chair and sat.

"What's on your mind?" Handler asked.

"I was just wondering," Clint said. "What brings a man like you all the way up here?"

"I heard the pickings would be easy," Handler said. "Not many gamblers would make this trip. In fact, there's only me and Jerry over there."

"I realize that, but are the pickings really that good?"

"To tell you the truth, no," Handler said. "It seems like the whores are getting to a lot of these men before I can."

"That's what I was figuring," Clint said.

"What about your partner? Does he play?"

"Ike? No, he's not a gambler. He holds on tight to every nugget he gets out of the ground."

"Too bad," Handler said. "Are you sure you don't want a game?"

"I'm sure," Clint said. "I didn't come up here to gamble . . . with cards anyway."

"Well, if you change your mind, I'll be here," Handler said. "Just don't give the kid over there first shot at you, okay?"

"Okay."

"And thanks for the beer."

"Sure."

Clint picked up his beer, stood up, and walked back to the bar.

TWENTY-FIVE

As Clint and Ike Daly walked into the saloon, Bent Miller and Hector Tailor were down the street, watching the Gunsmith and his partner from a distance.

Bent said to Hector, "I'm gonna kill him."

"Not today," Hector warned.

"No," Bent said, "not today, and not tomorrow. But I'm gonna be the one who does it."

"Well, make sure you wait for the word from me or Mr. Parker. That way you can kill the Gunsmith and get paid for it."

"Don't worry," Bent said. "I'm a patient man."

"Good," Hector said. "We'll need some buckboards to get this equipment to our site. I want you to take two of the men and go and get there."

"You want me to get the buckboards?"

"I can't let these men go off unsupervised," Hector told him. "They might never come back."

"Then I'll just take my two guys and we'll bring the buckboards back."

"Okay," Hector said. "However you want to do it, but we need them as soon as possible. Here." He handed Bent some money. "Rent them, don't buy them."

"Yessir, boss."

Bent went to get his two men, who weren't exactly happy about the idea.

"I was gonna go to the saloon," Billy Rohm said.

"I was headin' for the whorehouse," Ed Stash said.

"All that's gonna have to wait," Bent said. "You and me are gonna fetch some buckboards from town."

Rohm scratched his head, then said to Stash, "Well, we can locate the saloon and the whorehouse while we're gettin' the buckboards."

"We can hit them later, right?" Stash asked Bent.

"Once we get all the supplies to the camp, you guys can do whatever you want."

"Well, okay," Stash said. "Let's go."

"What about Adams?" Rohm asked as they walked to town. "When are you gonna take care of him?"

"Don't you worry about that," Bent said. "I'll do that when the time is right."

"And when's that?"

"When I say it's time," Bent Miller said. "Now stop talkin' about Adams, or maybe I'll just send you two guys after him."

"Not me," Stash said. "I don't want no part of the Gunsmith."

"Me neither," Rohm said. "He's all yours, Bent."

* * *

Clint came out of the saloon and saw Bent Miller walking past with two men. Miller simply inclined his head in a greeting that Clint returned. Clint didn't know where they were going, but it was probably on some errand for Hector Tailor. Clint thought the young man was showing more sand than he ever thought he'd have.

"Who's that?" somebody asked from behind him.

He turned and looked. It was one of the saloon girls, and she had crept up behind him as quiet as a cat. It was the kind of carelessness he rarely displayed. If she'd had a knife, he would have been in trouble.

"His name's Bent Miller," Clint said. "I don't know the other two."

"Bent," she said. "I heard of him. He's supposed to be a bad man."

"That's what I've heard."

"I heard of you, too."

"Have you?"

She folded her arms beneath somewhat chubby breasts and said, "Everyone has. You're the Gunsmith."

"And what's your name?"

"Lori."

"What brought you up here?"

She shrugged. "Somethin' to do. I didn't have much of a life to leave behind."

"That seems to be the reason most people come up here."

"What about you?"

"Me? I'm doing a favor for a friend."

"That funny little fella I see you with?"

"Yes."

"It's a long way to come for a friend."

Now Clint shrugged, not knowing what to say to that.

"You go to the whores?" she asked.

"No," he said. "I don't pay for women."

She studied him for a moment, then said, "No, you wouldn't have to. Well, I don't take money from men, but it gets real cold up here at night. I've got my own tent behind this place. Come and see me. We'll snuggle and . . . get warm."

She had light brown hair, a fine body that was starting to go soft in her thirties—which to Clint wasn't a bad thing.

"I might just take you up on that offer."

She smiled, unfolded her arms, and said, "You won't be sorry."

She went back into the saloon.

TWENTY-SIX

Clint worked the rest of the day with Ike and the men at the river, all using sluice boxes to pan for gold nuggets.

Clint hadn't told Ike, but when they arrived and saw Ike's "claim," he was disappointed. He was also disappointed with what they were getting out of the river. Behind them, up a slope, equipment was being installed that would allow them to excavate the ground, looking for veins of gold. Of course, the deeper you went, the better chance you had of finding it. They didn't have the kind of equipment Calvin Parker had sent up the river.

At the end of the day, Ike was pleased with the take. He told the men they could head for the saloon or the whorehouse, whichever they preferred.

"What about you?" Ike asked Clint.

"Saloon," Clint said, "and then I think I'm going to visit a friend."

"A friend?"

Clint nodded. "For the night."

* * *

When Clint got to the saloon, it was busier than he'd
seen it before. The poker games were in full swing, and
so were the fights. The men who weren't gambling or
fighting were drinking with both hands.

Many of the miners who were actually getting gold
out of the ground were spending it just as quickly. Every
night the whores in town were kept busy. And the saloon
girls had to run their legs off to keep the miners drinking so they wouldn't have time to fight.

And while inside the saloon the pickpockets were at
work, outside drunken miners were being tolled for the
nuggets or dust they had left.

Ike told Clint he'd meet him at the saloon when he
was done with one of the whores.

"Might take me a while to pick one, though," he said.
"I don't have a type. I like 'em all."

"Don't worry," Clint said. "I'll be there until they
close." Where else would he go? There was nothing else
to do. The only other way to spend time was reading in
his tent. This was why he couldn't have spent his life as
a miner, the way Ike had. In fact, he'd already been at
it longer than ever before. He was thinking that once he
and Ike got the operation up and running, it would be
time for him to leave Alaska. Ike could handle the whole
operation, and send his share to a bank in Texas.

Bent Miller ducked his head and entered Hector Tailor's
tent. Tailor had two lamps going, and had set a table up
in the center. He had the plans for their mining operation spread out on it.

"This isn't good," he said to Bent.

"What?"

Hector pointed.

"Our claim butts right up against Ike Daly's."

"And you didn't know that when we came up here?" Bent asked.

"No," Hector said, "we didn't."

"Well, that's a big coincidence," Bent said.

"Ike doesn't have the biggest claim along the Forty Mile," Hector said. "Ours is the biggest, but between us, I think we have the two richest."

"I know what that means," Bent said.

"What?"

"Your boss wants their claim."

"Well, if he knew what I know, yes, he'd want it," Hector said. "So I'm going to make it happen."

"I guess that means I'm going to make it happen," Bent Miller said.

Hector abandoned the plans, turned, and faced Bent.

"I have an idea."

"Time to kill the Gunsmith?"

"No," Hector said. "The Gunsmith is not the driving force behind that claim."

"You mean . . ."

"Ike Daly," Hector said. "If he was dead, Adams would lose interest. He'd sell out."

"Not if he knew we killed his friend."

"That's why it has to look like this place killed him," Hector said. "There are enough pickpockets, grifters, and thieves up here."

"All I have to do is make it look like he was killed while being robbed."

"Exactly."

"When do you want it to happen?" Bent asked.

"The sooner the better," Hector said. "Tonight wouldn't be out of line."

"I'll have to find him," Bent said. "I better get started. The whores would be a good bet. Where will you be?"

"Right here."

"Might be a better idea if you were in the saloon," Bent said, "where everyone can see you."

"Good point."

"I'll go there with you," Bent said, "and then slip out the back. It'll be so crowded I'll just need to put in an appearance, make sure I'm seen, and then slip out."

"All right," Hector said. "Let me get my coat."

"And buy drinks for people," Bent said as they left the tent. "Lots and lots of drinks."

TWENTY-SEVEN

Clint got himself a spot at the bar when he arrived, and held on to it after that. He was not lured away by the poker games, or the girls. He was saving himself for Lori, who came by every so often to talk to him, and remind him of their appointment by touching him with her hands, or bumping him with her hip.

He was standing with his back to the bar, holding his beer, when Hector Tailor and Bent Miller entered. They looked around, and even in the crowded interior, they spotted him. However, they made sure to go to the other end of the bar, which suited him.

Bent Miller made room at the bar for himself and Hector. When a man turned to see who had bumped into him, Bent gave him a long, hard look that made the man take his beer and abandon his position.

"Two beers," Bent said to the bartender.

"Comin' up."

When the beers came, he handed one to Hector, then observed the room.

"Make friends," he said.

Hector frowned.

"That's not something I'm good at."

"Just talk to the guy next to you," Bent said. "Walk around, talk to some of the girls. And mention me, like I'm still here."

"Okay. What are you going to do?"

"I'll walk around, mingle, finish my beer, and then slip out the back."

"Okay."

"And I'll have to come back when I'm finished," Bent said. "The night has to end with both of us still here."

"I understand."

"Okay, then," Bent said. "I'll see you back here later tonight."

"How are you going to do it?" Hector asked.

"By not staying here answering that question," Bent said. "Do you really care how it's done?"

"No," Hector said, "no, I don't. Just get it done, Bent."

"All right," Bent said, "but while I'm gone, there's one thing you have to do."

"What?"

"Talk to Clint Adams."

TWENTY-EIGHT

Clint was surprised when Hector Tailor came walking up to him.

"How are you?" the man asked rather awkwardly.

"I'm fine," Clint said. "Where's Miller?"

The question seemed to startle Hector.

"He's in here somewhere, with a beer," Hector said. "I, uh, saw him talking to one of the girls."

"This isn't a place I expected to see you," Clint commented. "You struck me as the type who's all work and no play."

"Well, you know," Hector said. "You've got to take some time out once in a while, and what else is there to do here?"

"There are always the whores."

"I'd like to be able to take my time off without catching a disease," Hector said. "I just need a beer or two, and then I can go back to work."

"How's it coming?" Clint asked.

"Pretty well," Hector said.

"Mr. Parker must have a lot of faith in you, sending you up here without him."

"He knows he can trust me to oversee operations."

"With Miller along for . . . help?"

"Sometimes you just need someone who can get things done," Hector pointed out.

"That's a fact," Clint said. "You do need somebody like that around sometimes."

"Well, nice talking to you," Hector said, and drifted away.

"Who was that?" Lori asked, coming up alongside Clint.

"Somebody trying to be something he's not," Clint said. He looked around, trying to locate Bent Miller.

"Looked like he was just trying to be friendly," she said.

"That's exactly what I mean," Clint said. "He's not the type."

"He looks kind of buttoned down," she said.

"Exactly," Clint said. "Do me a favor, will you?"

"Of course. What is it?"

"Have one of your girlfriends cuddle up to him."

She laughed.

"You want her to see if he'll panic?"

"Something like that, yeah."

"I know just the girl," Lori said. "She loves playing with men's heads."

"Good," Clint said. "Let's have some fun."

* * *

Bent Miller finished his beer by the time he worked his way to the rear of the saloon. He put his mug down and slipped out the back.

He knew where the whores were because he'd checked it out when he first arrived. He kept to the darkness as he worked his way to the row of tents the girls used. From the sounds coming from inside, all the tents were busy. He felt sure Ike Daly was in one of them. All he had to do now was wait.

Ike stared down at the girl's head as she bobbed up and down on his hard cock. He was far from a lady's man, and the only time he was ever with a woman was when he paid one. But he didn't care. That was what money—and gold—was for. And he had taken enough dust out of the ground that day to pay this young lady for what she was doing, and still go to the saloon and drink with Clint afterward.

The blond head kept bobbing up and down until finally Ike lifted his butt off the cot he was sitting on and exploded into her mouth.

"Aw, damn!" he shouted.

She sat back on her haunches and smiled up at him.

Bent heard several cries of delight from inside the tents. He knew the girls liked to get men in and out as quickly as they could, so somebody was going to be coming out soon. That was when he saw somebody else creeping around in the dark. This was not the kind of work he usually did, but there were those who did this for a living. He was sure the other figure in the dark was working, too.

He located the shape again, then moved up behind it. Turned out to be a smaller man than him. It was a simple thing to clamp his arm around the guy's throat and squeeze, cutting off his air.

"Sorry, friend," he said into the man's ear, "I don't need you plying your trade out here tonight."

He squeezed until the man went limp, then dragged him into the dark behind a tent and set him down on the ground. He only hoped this little detour hadn't caused him to miss Ike Daly.

Ike Daly pulled up his pants and said to the girl, "That was great, Christy. I'll be back again tomorrow night."

"You're always welcome, Ike," she said, "as long as you bring some more of that gold dust."

Ike left, and Christy deposited his dust into a bag with the batch she got from all the other men. She wasn't doing any of the panning or the digging, but she was still working hard on her knees—and back—for her gold.

Ike left Christy's tent and headed in the direction of the saloon. Before he could get away from the rows of whores' tents, he was grabbed from behind and a knife punched him in the back. He jerked like he'd been electrocuted, and then went limp. He was dragged into the dark, his pockets rifled, and the remains of the gold he had in his poke was removed. It might have been more profitable to grab Ike—or any man—before they went into the tents, but they were a lot more relaxed and careless when they came out.

Ike's body was left behind the tents, where the cold would keep it until someone stumbled over it.

TWENTY-NINE

It was getting late and Clint wondered where Ike was. He knew his friend was pretty quick when he went to visit the girls. He usually spent more time over a cold beer.

He looked around, saw Hector with a chubby blond girl pressed up against him. The man's face looked panicked. The girl had been cuddling up to him ever since Lori pulled her aside and spoke to her. Hector looked like he wanted to bolt and run, but he didn't. Clint thought he knew why.

He was waiting for Miller.

Miller walked into the saloon through the back door. His empty mug was still where he'd left it. He picked it up and headed for the bar. Along the way he saw Hector with a girl scaring the hell out of him. Miller laughed, and kept walking until he got to the bar. He exchanged the empty mug for a full one.

* * *

Hector had no use for the blond girl, and kept trying to tell her so, but she insisted on attaching herself to him. He figured it must have been the aura of power he gave off. He wished Bent Miller would return so he could get back to work. He didn't see how men could spend all their time in an environment like this.

Before rescuing Hector, Miller decided to talk to Clint Adams.

Clint saw Miller coming toward him with a full mug of beer. The man was heading directly for him, obviously with something on his mind.

"Buy you a beer?" Miller asked.

"Working on my last one," Clint said, raising his half-filled mug, "but thanks."

"Maybe tomorrow night, then."

"Sure."

Miller looked over at Hector.

"That girl is scaring him to death," he said. "You pay her to do it?"

"I didn't have to pay her," Clint said. "We were just having some fun with your boss."

"Yeah, well, I better get him back to camp before he craps his pants."

"Might have to get a drink into him first."

"Yeah, well, he's not a real hard drinker either," Miller said. "Buy you that beer tomorrow night, Adams."

"Yeah, see you."

Bent Miller left Clint and walked over to Hector. Clint didn't really see any reason for the conversation. He watched the two men carefully.

* * *

When Hector saw Bent Miller coming toward him, he breathed a sigh of relief.

"I'm sorry," he said to the girl, "I have to go."

"You sure, honey?" she asked. "We were just gettin' friendly."

"Yeah, sorry," Hector said. "I've got a lot of work I need to do in the morning. Good night, ma'am."

The girl released her hold on his arm and smiled as the man almost ran toward his friend, who was shaking his head and laughing.

As Hector reached Bent, he asked, "What took you so long?"

"You sure you don't wanna stay with your girlfriend?" Bent teased him.

"She's not my girlfriend," Hector retorted, not getting the joke. "She just attached herself to me for some reason."

"Must be the power," Bent commented.

"That's what I thought," Hector said, still not getting the joke.

"Yeah, right," Bent said. "Come on, have another drink and then we'll go."

"I don't want a drink," Hector said. "I want to get out of here. How did it go?"

"Let's get back to camp," Bent said, "and then we've got something to talk about."

Bent gave his beer mug to a passing girl, and he and Hector left the saloon.

Lori and her friend, Beth, came up to Clint.

"Was that what you wanted?" Beth asked.

"That was it," Clint said.

"I think I scared him pretty good."

"Let me give you something for your trouble," Clint offered.

"Money?" Beth asked. "I don't want your money, honey. Maybe we can figure out another way for you to pay me, though."

"Oh, no," Lori said, placing herself between Beth and Clint. "He's mine tonight."

"You could share, Lori," Beth said. "After all, we're friends. What do you think, handsome?"

Beth looked to be Lori's age, a little on the plump size, which always worked for Clint in bed.

"Well . . ." he said.

"Maybe another night, Beth," Lori said. "This is the first night for me and Clint, and I want him all to myself."

"Well, too bad," she said to Clint, "but I'll be available tomorrow night . . . or any night. Come and see me."

"Maybe I'll do that," Clint said.

Lori latched on to his arm as Beth walked away and said, "And maybe you won't."

THIRTY

When Ike didn't come back to the saloon, Clint assumed he had gone right back to the camp. Since he had already told him he wouldn't be back at camp that night, Ike wouldn't be worried about him either.

Clint waited outside the saloon while it emptied out, and then Lori came out with Beth and another girl.

"Are you ready?" she asked.

"I'm ready to get warm," he said.

"Oh, you'll get warm," she said.

"Are you sure you don't need help warmin' him up?" Beth asked.

"I'm sure," Lori said. "Good night, girls."

"Good night," Beth said, and she and the other girl walked off.

"My tent's back here," Lori said.

She took his hand and led him around behind the saloon. There was a tent there, with no others around it.

"Wouldn't you feel safer with some of the other girls around you?" he asked.

"No," she said. "We'd look like a bunch of whores livin' in a row of tents. I like this better. Nobody around me."

"Aren't you scared?"

"I've got a gun in my tent," she said, "and I know how to use it."

They got to the tent. She held the flap aside while he went in, then she entered and let it down. He stood still in the dark while she lit a lamp. He looked around. There was no cot, just a bed of blankets on the ground with a cold fire in front of it, and some stones.

"You stay dry in here?" he asked, looking around.

"Oh yeah," she said. "It's been rain tested, believe me."

It was large enough for the two of them, for her to stand and him to stoop slightly.

"How do you stay warm?"

"I build a small fire, and the fire heats the stones. It works pretty good."

She took off her jacket, then hunkered down and tossed some pieces of wood into the cold fire.

"Got a match?" she asked. "I usually do it without one, but . . ."

He took out a wooden lucifer and handed it to her. She flicked it and lit the fire. The wood burned and he could immediately feel the heat.

She looked up at him and smiled.

"We'll give the stones time to heat up," she said, "and then we can get naked without freezing."

"Sounds good."

He crouched down next to her.

"I'll make some coffee," she said.

"Good."

Before she did that, though, she leaned over and kissed him. The kiss went on for a long time, but they kept their hands down. They both wanted this to go slow.

"That was nice," she said.

"Yes, it was."

She reached into a shadowy corner and came out with a coffeepot.

"There's a stream behind us," she said, handing him the pot. "Why don't you get us some water for the coffee?"

"Okay."

He stood up, went outside, and walked back to where he could hear the stream running. There was enough moonlight for him to see. He crouched by the stream, let the pot fill, then turned and walked back to the tent.

Hector and Bent Miller got back to their camp. In Hector's tent they started a fire and put on a pot of coffee. The tent was very large, with plenty of room for them, a cot, and a table. A lamp hung from the center, and there were two more off to the side.

Bent Miller had his own tent, half this size, which was fine for him. But for now, they would stay in Hector's tent to drink coffee and discuss the evening's events.

"Is it done?" Hector asked.

"Well, let's put it this way," Bent said, "it got done. Ike Daly is dead."

"How'd you do it?"

"That's just it. I didn't do it," he said truthfully. "Somebody else did."

"What are you talking about?"

"There was a guy sneaking around out there that I took care of. He was obviously waiting for some of the miners to finish with the whores. But while I was dealing with him, somebody else was killing Daly."

"But who?"

"Who knows?" Bent asked. "There are lots of thieves in this camp. Any one of them coulda done it. All I know is that when I found him, he was lying on the ground, already dead."

"Okay," Hector said, shrugging. "Daly's dead, and that's what counts."

"So what do we do now?" Bent asked.

"Now," Hector said, "we just wait. Coffee?" He held out the pot.

"That's okay," Bent said. "I'm going back to my tent to get some sleep. See you in the morning."

"Okay," Hector said. "Good night."

Bent left.

Bent Miller went to his own tent, lit his lamp. He had a cot, and that was it. He also had room to build a small fire for heat. He had seen Stash and Rohm in the saloon, but he had let them be. He didn't need his men for what he was going to do.

He lit a lamp, sat on his cot, and lit a cigarette.

Clint brought the pot of water back into the tent and Lori tossed some grounds into it.

"More," Clint said.

"More?"

"I like it strong."

"Okay," she said, "more."

She tossed in another handful and put the pot on the fire, then they sat down on the ground with their shoulders touching to wait for it to be ready.

THIRTY-ONE

Clint and Lori drank their coffee, warming their insides while their outsides were also warming up. Before long it was warm enough for Clint to take off his jacket.

"You always wear that gun?" she asked.

"All the time."

"Why?"

"To stay alive."

"Wait," she said, "you told me your name was . . . Clint?"

"That's right."

"Clint . . . Adams?"

"Smart girl."

"Jesus," she said, "I didn't realize you were . . . the Gunsmith."

"That's okay," Clint said. "I'm fine with that."

"But what are you doin' all the way up here?" she asked.

"What everyone else is doing," he said, "looking for gold."

"You said that before, but you don't seem the type."

"Well, like I've said a few times before, I'm doing it for my friend Ike."

"So how long will you stay?" she asked.

"Not much longer."

"I've seen you in the saloon before. I guess I should have come up to you sooner."

"Yes, you should."

He leaned over and kissed her this time. Again, it went on for a while and did not include hands.

"Whew," she said, "it's starting to get really warm in here, isn't it?"

"It sure is."

They put their cups down and began to unbutton each other's shirts. Clint slid hers off, saw how pale her skin was. Her breasts were large and firm, the nipples brown and very long, distended either by passion or cold, or both.

She slid his shirt off his shoulders, leaned forward, and kissed his chest. He, in turn, kissed her smooth shoulders, giving her chills that had nothing to do with the cold.

"Are you gonna wear that gun the whole time?" she asked.

He unstrapped the gun belt and laid it aside, but within reach.

Bent Miller had a bottle of whiskey in his tent. He opened it and drank directly from it. He didn't know what the hell he was doing in Alaska. Gold was never something he had a hankering for, but it was the lure of gold that brought him here, just like everyone else. Now he wanted to go home. It was too cold here. Too damn cold.

But he was here, so he was going to do his job, and he was going to make some money. And make some money for his boys, Rohm and Stash.

He stood up, wondered if he should go and find a woman, but he really didn't need that kind of trouble either.

He sat back down and drank.

Hector Tailor doused his light and reclined down on his cot. Tomorrow was going to be a big day. Providing somebody found Ike Daly's body.

He needed a good night's rest to deal with it all.

Clint and Lori finished undressing each other. They rolled themselves up in her blanket bed, pressed tightly together, enjoying each other's warmth. Clint usually enjoyed sex without covers, but he did have to make some concessions to being in a tent in Alaska.

Lori reached between them to grasp his hard penis and stroke it. He slid one hand down between her legs and kissed her while he used one finger to probe her wet pussy. She moaned into his mouth and lifted her hips to meet the pressure of his hand. She reached her hand even lower to stroke and fondle his sensitive testicles. Finally, she couldn't wait anymore. She grasped his cock more firmly and guided him to her. He touched her with the head of his penis and she spread her legs as much as she could within the confines of the blanket. He entered her and found her to be like an oven.

She moaned again and lifted her hips to him. He slid his hands beneath her to cup her butt cheeks and pull her to him as he fucked her. His nostrils filled with the smell of her, and their bare flesh began to become dappled with perspiration. However, they couldn't cast off the blankets, for the cold Alaska night air would probably have frozen their sweat in place.

They continued to lunge at each other within their blanketed cocoon until she shuddered, and he erupted inside her . . .

THIRTY-TWO

When Clint got back to camp the next morning and didn't find Ike there, he started to worry. He went out and found Dallas and Jud preparing to go down to the river to start the day's work.

"Have you seen Ike?"

"Not this mornin'," Dallas said.

"I think he was with a whore last night," Jud said. "Maybe he stayed with her."

"These whores don't usually take in customers for the night," Clint said, "but I'll go and check. See you boys later."

Clint left camp.

Bent Miller woke and came out of his tent, rubbing his face. Billy Rohm and Ed Stash were standing by the fire, drinking coffee. Rohm poured a cup and handed it to Bent. As he looked around, he did not see Hector Tailor yet.

"What did you boys get up to last night?" he asked.

"Whores!" Stash said with a grin.

"More than one!" Rohm said, also grinning.

"Those girls are diseased," Bent said.

"Mebbe," Stash said, "but what a way to die."

Bent looked around camp. Men were getting themselves together for the day's work. Some would pan the river, but others were busy erecting the equipment that would help turn this into a proper mining operation.

Finally, Hector came out of his tent. He walked over, but no one poured any coffee for him, so he poured his own.

Stash and Rohm found something else to do. They did not like Hector, and chose not to deal with him. They only spoke and dealt with Bent Miller, whom they considered to be their boss.

"Hearing anything about last night?" Hector asked.

"No, but I just came out myself," Bent said. "There's been no time for him to be found yet."

"What do you think Adams will do when they do find him?"

"No way of knowing," Bent said. "If Daly's the only reason he's here, he might take the next boat out."

"That would suit me." Hector drank some coffee. "Why don't you see what you can find out today."

"Yeah, okay."

"I'll be in my tent, working."

Those damn plans, Bent thought. Hector spent most of his time leaning over them.

"I'm gonna get some breakfast in town, too," Bent said. He tossed the remnants of his coffee into the flames, causing them to flare.

"Suit yourself," Hector said. "Just report to me later."

Bent didn't like the idea of "reporting" to Hector, but he said, "Yeah, okay," and left camp.

Marshal Sean Casey asked Trooper Allan Craig, "Is that the town up ahead?"

No structures were yet in sight, but there were several tendrils of smoke rising into the air.

"That would be it," Craig said.

"How much of a town is it?" Casey asked.

"Not much, I would guess," Craig said. "Made up mostly of tents."

"And no law?"

"No," Craig said. "There's just us."

"Well," Casey said, "let's get down there. We got a killer to catch."

THIRTY-THREE

It was raining by the time Clint reached the town of Forty Mile, and already the streets were turning muddy. If it continued to rain into the evening when the temperatures dropped, it would turn to snow.

He reached the row of whores' tents, started at the first one. He knew he was waking up the hardworking girls, but for the most part they were cooperative once they realized he wasn't looking for an early morning poke.

It wasn't till he got to the fifth tent that he found the right girl.

"Christy," she said. "My name's Christy, and yeah, I know Ike. He comes to see me sometimes. Why? What happened?"

"I haven't seen him this morning," Clint said. "Was he with you last night?"

"Yeah, but just for a little while," she said.

"Where did he say he was going when he left?"

"To the saloon."

"Well, he never got there, and he never came back to camp," Clint said. "I'll have to keep looking."

"I hope you find him," she said. He thought she sounded concerned, until her next line. "I can't really afford to lose regular customers."

"Yeah," he said. "I'll let you know."

She pulled her thin wrap tightly around her and withdrew into the warmth of her tent.

Clint talked to the rest of the girls, but none of them had seen Ike.

He walked the distance between the row of tents and the saloon, but didn't come across him or anyone who had seen him.

He did come across something else, though. Two men riding tired-looking horses into town. He was surprised to see Marshal Casey and Trooper Craig.

They, however, were not surprised to see him as they reined in their horses in front of the saloon, which was always open.

"Adams," Casey said, stepping down from his horse.

"You two rode all the way here from Skagway?" Clint asked.

"The trooper knew the way," Casey said. "In fact, he says it was a shorter way than most, but it took a lot of ridin'."

"Mr. Adams," Craig said.

"Nice to see you, Trooper."

"Does this saloon serve coffee?" Casey asked.

"It does all day, and if you don't mind, I'll join you."

"Fine," Casey said. "You can fill us in on the situation here."

"And you can tell me what brought you all the way here from Skagway."

"Agreed."

The three men went into the saloon.

Bent Miller stopped short when he saw the two lawmen ride in. He secreted himself behind a tent and watched as they met with Clint Adams in front of the saloon. The men talked for a while, and then the three men went inside.

He came out from behind the tent and walked toward the saloon, wondering if Clint Adams had yet found the body of his friend, Ike Daly.

He stopped just outside the saloon and peered inside. The three men were standing at the bar, and he watched.

THIRTY-FOUR

Clint, Casey, and Craig all got coffee mugs from the bartender.

"So what brings you here?"

"Murder," Trooper Craig said.

"Who was murdered?" Clint asked.

"A whore," Marshal Casey said. "Poor girl was brutalized."

"Her name was Francesca something," Craig said. "They called her Frankie."

"Frankie?" Clint asked, alarmed. "Frankie's dead?"

"You knew her?" Casey asked.

"I came over on the boat with her," Clint said. "A nice girl. I let her sleep in my cabin, so she wouldn't have to sleep on deck."

The two lawmen exchanged a glance, but Clint let them think whatever they liked.

"Did you see her at all in Skagway?" Casey asked.

"No," Clint said. "In fact, I didn't know she was a

whore until we got to the dock and one of the other girls met her."

"Well," Casey said, "according to the madam, she'd only been with one man."

"What man was that?"

"Bent Miller," Craig said. "He has a reputation for brutality. The madam thinks he did it. She said he'd never killed a girl before, but he'd hurt them badly."

"Do you know where he is?" Casey asked.

"He works out at the Parker mining operation," Clint said. "I think he's the foreman."

"Never heard that Miller was a miner," Craig said. "Mostly, he's a gun for hire."

"That's what I thought," Clint said, "but he's apparently the number two to Parker's man, Hector Tailor."

"I suppose we'll have to go out and question both of them, then," Craig said.

"Maybe we can get something to eat first," Casey said.

"There's a tent just down the way from here serves pretty good food," Clint said. "Just go out and turn left."

"And what about a place to stay?" Casey asked.

"If you go to the mercantile tent, they'll rent you a tent, any size you want. Then you'll just have to find a place to pitch it."

"No hotel?" Casey asked.

"No hotel," Clint said.

Casey frowned into his coffee.

Craig put his empty mug down on the bar.

"Let's see to our horses first," he suggested to the U.S. marshal.

"Down at the end of the street is the livery," Clint

said. "This and the livery are really the only wooden structures in town so far."

"Well," Casey said, "at least the horses will be comfortable."

Bent Miller saw all three men push away from the bar and turn toward the exit. He withdrew, found a place to hide himself as the three men came outside. From where he was, he could hear them now.

"All right," the marshal was saying, "we'll deal with the horses, get something to eat, then go out to the Parker operation to talk to Tailor and Miller."

"Sounds like a plan," Clint said.

"What else is going on up here?" Craig asked.

"Well, nothing that requires a lawman," Clint said, "except that I'm still trying to find my partner this morning."

"The little guy?" Casey asked.

"Ike Daly," Clint said. "Haven't seen him since last night."

"Well," Craig said, "let us know if you need any help."

"Not that we don't have enough to do," Casey added.

"I'll keep it in mind," Clint said.

The two lawmen went to their horses and mounted up. As Clint watched them ride off, Bent Miller watched Clint. Once the lawmen were gone, Clint started walking in the direction of the whores' tents.

Bent Miller decided to go ahead and get something to eat. He did not have any doubt that he could handle the two lawmen, and he wasn't going to let their presence ruin his breakfast.

* * *

Clint went back toward the tents, intending to look around with more care. With the number of rounders and lowlifes in this kind of town, there was no telling what might have happened.

He walked along in front of the tents, then went around to the back. It was there he finally found his friend, facedown in a puddle. At that moment the rain began to come down even harder.

THIRTY-FIVE

Clint leaned down and turned his friend over. His face was pale. He'd been dead all night. He rolled him again, saw where the knife had gone in. Searching him, he found his friend's poke gone. This would indicate a robbery, but there was no guarantee of that. However it had happened, though, his friend was dead. Murdered. Coincidentally on the day the two lawmen rode into town.

"Ah, Ike," he said with his hand still on his friend.

He had come out of Christy's tent, probably intending to go to the saloon to meet Clint, and had, instead, met his end.

Well, since there was *law* in town, he figured he might as well let those lawmen know that they now had two killings—one in Skagway and the other in Forty Mile—to deal with. But he also needed to figure out where Ike's body should be taken, and then find someone to pick him up and take him there.

He hated to leave his friend where he was, but it would only be for a little while longer.

He headed back toward town to find the lawmen.

Bent Miller was seated, eating his breakfast, when Marshal Casey and Trooper Craig entered. If they saw him, they didn't let on. Instead, they went to an empty table and ordered some food for themselves.

"He's here," Craig said as they sat down.

"Who?" Casey asked.

"Miller," Craig said, then added, "Don't look."

"I don't know where to look," Casey said. "And right now I'm more interested in some food. I don't think Miller's going anywhere, do you?"

"No," Craig said. "There's nowhere else to go."

A waiter came over and they both ordered ham and eggs and coffee. The waiter promised the food would come quickly, and he didn't lie. He was back in moments with two steaming plates, a pot of coffee, and a basket of fresh biscuits.

"This is good," Craig said.

"If it was the soles of a boot cooked in grease, it would taste good after eating your cookin' on the trail."

"What's wrong with my cooking?"

"It can't even be called cookin'," Casey said. He pointed to his plate with his fork. "This is cookin'."

"I can't argue with you there," Craig said.

They were busily consuming their meals when Clint Adams came through the door.

Clint saw Bent Miller first, then the two lawmen at another table, wolfing down their food.

As Clint approached their table, Casey asked, "You have some news so soon?"

"I found Ike Daly," Clint said. "He's dead. He was stabbed sometime last night."

"Was he robbed?" Craig asked.

"It looks like it," Clint said.

"Looks like it?" Casey asked. "You think it was something else?"

"I don't know," Clint said. "All I know is, he's dead. I thought I'd let you know."

As Clint started walking away from the table, Casey said, "Now wait. Where are you off to?"

"I need to arrange to have his body taken out of the mud," Clint said, "and then I'm going to find his killer."

"You're going to find his killer?" Craig asked. "What about us?"

"You fellas can help, if you like," Clint said.

"I think you got this backwards, Adams," Casey said. "Murder is our business, and if you want, you can help *us* find the killer."

"Whichever way it goes," Clint said, "I've got to get his body moved."

"Wait," Craig said, standing. "I'll come with you. I want to see the body where you found it."

Casey looked down at the remainder of his breakfast with distress.

"Marshal, you might as well stay here and finish your breakfast," Craig said.

"But—"

"No, no," Craig said, "this will only take one of us. Besides, maybe you can talk to Miller before you leave."

"That's not a bad idea," Casey said. "Okay, let's meet at the mercantile in an hour."

"Agreed," Craig said. "Then he looked at Clint. "Come on, show me where you found your friend."

"Daly," Clint said. "His name is Ike Daly."

"Yes," Craig said, "my apologies. Show me where you found Mr. Daly."

As they left, Casey looked across the table, then figured there was no point in the rest of the trooper's breakfast going to waste. He picked up the plate and scraped the remaining food off onto his own, then continued eating.

THIRTY-SIX

Clint walked Trooper Craig around to where Ike's body lay.

"Did you move him?"

"I rolled him over to make sure it was him."

Craig crouched near the body.

"Search him?"

"Yeah," Clint said. "That's how I know his poke is gone."

"Looks like a stab wound," Craig said, touching the body right near the wound. "Only one apparently. None in front?"

"No."

Craig stood up.

"He was with a whore last night?"

"Yes, Christy. I spoke with her. She said she thought he was going to the saloon when he left her."

"Some of these whores partner with the thieves,"

Craig said. "They pass the word about who's got a good-sized poke."

"That's possible," Clint said. "Ike wasn't shy about taking his out of his pocket."

"I'll talk to her," Craig said. "You might as well go ahead and arrange for the body to be picked up."

"And you?"

"I'm going to look around, ask some questions." Craig said. "If you like, you can meet the marshal and me over at the mercantile in an hour."

"I'll be there," Clint said.

The two men parted company there.

Casey was still eating when Bent Miller stood up and started to leave.

"Mr. Miller."

Bent stopped and looked around.

"Sean Casey, U.S, marshal," Casey introduced himself. "You mind if we have a word?"

"About what?"

"A dead whore in Skagway."

"What's that got to do with me?"

"Why don't you have a seat," Casey suggested, "and we'll talk about it."

"Why not?" Miller said, sitting down.

"How much time do you spend with whores, Mr. Miller?" Casey asked.

"About as much time as anybody, I guess," Bent said. "What about you, Marshal? You like whores?"

"I like women," Casey said, "but I don't particularly like whores."

"I like 'em because they do what you pay 'em to do," Bent said. "That saves a lot of time and argument, don't you think?"

"I wouldn't call that any kind of relationship with a woman," Casey said.

"I don't want a relationship," Bent said, "I just want 'em to do what I say."

"And if they don't?"

"Then they don't get paid."

"That's it?" Casey asked.

"Whataya mean?"

"I mean, if they don't do what you say, is that all you do to them? Not pay them?"

"Ah, you been hearin' stories about me," Bent said. "You can't believe stories that you hear, Marshal."

"So you don't have a reputation for brutalizing whores?"

"I may have a reputation," Bent said, "but I ain't earned it. Maybe I slapped one or two of 'em around, but that ain't brutalizin' them."

"What would you call it?"

"Just givin' 'em a little . . . discipline. Ain't that what married men do with their wives? Keep 'em in line?"

"By hitting them?"

Bent Miller shrugged and said, "That's what my pa used to do when my ma got outta line. One little slap usually did it. There was no reason to do anything more. Not like what you're talkin' about."

"I see."

"I'm sorry about the girl who got killed, I really am," Bent said, "but that's just a waste of a whore."

"What about Ike Daly?"

"What about him?"

"Did you hear that he got killed last night?"

"Naw," Bent said, "really? That's too bad. What happened? He get robbed or somethin'?"

"Why would you say that?"

"Well, a lot of that goes around in a place like this," Bent said. "You know, some fellas just don't wanna do the hard work of gettin' the gold outta the ground. They wait 'til somebody else gets it, and then steal it away."

"We're not sure exactly what happened," Casey said. "But if that's what did happen, then somebody went a bit too far this time."

"Sounds like they did," Bent said. "And I'm sorry to hear about that."

"I'm sure Mr. Adams will be glad to hear that," Casey said. "You wouldn't have any ideas about who might have done it, would you?"

"Nope, sorry," Bent said. "Like I said, I know it goes on, but I don't know who's doin' it."

"Okay, then," Casey said. "Thanks for talkin' to me, Mr. Miller."

"Sure thing, Marshal," Bent said, standing up. "You have a nice day."

As Miller went out the door, Casey wondered why the man had not been surprised to see him in Forty Mile, and why he hadn't asked him when he'd arrived. It seemed as if Miller had already known that he was in town.

He paid his bill, put his hat on, and stepped outside.

He still had some time before he had to meet Craig at the mercantile. Maybe he could find something out by asking questions around town.

He headed out into the rain.

THIRTY-SEVEN

Clint couldn't find anyone who would help with Ike's body. And apparently, there was no undertaker to take it to. There was a boot hill cemetery right outside of town, and it seemed that folks just took the dead directly out there and buried the bodies themselves.

Clint went to the livery and rented a buckboard and horse, then drove it over to where Ike's body lay. He picked his friend up and laid him on the buckboard, then drove him to their camp.

"What happened?" Dallas asked.

"Somebody killed him last night," Clint said.

The men crowded around and looked at Ike's body on the buckboard.

"Anybody see anything last night?" Clint said. "Anything that might help?"

"Didn't even see him last night," Jud said. "I just thought he found himself a real good whore."

"Me, too," Dallas said.

"Well, it was after he left the whore that he was killed," Clint said. "And robbed."

"Aw, poor Ike," Dallas said. "He never hurt anybody."

"What do we do with him?" Jud asked.

"We'll have to bury him," Clint said, "but not on boot hill. Near here, I think. Near his claim."

"There's a nice spot just above here, in some trees," Jud said.

"Show me," Clint said.

Clint followed Jud up a hill till they reached the point Jud was talking about. Below them was the running Forty Mile River.

"This is a good spot, Jud," Clint said. "He'd have picked this out himself."

"I'll get a couple of guys with shovels to dig the hole, Clint," Jud said.

"I'll go down and get the body ready," Clint said.

They came down the hill together, then split up. Clint went over to the buckboard, where Dallas was still standing.

"Okay," Clint said, "we've got the spot."

"Should we find somebody to build a coffin?" Dallas asked.

"No," Clint said, "we'll wrap him in blankets, Ike wouldn't have wanted a box. Jud's having some men dig the grave."

"I'll go and help," Dallas said.

"Meet me back down here," Clint said.

He watched Dallas walk up the hill, then went in search of a bunch of blankets.

* * *

They got Ike buried on the hill overlooking the river. There was no clergy in Forty Mile, so Clint said a few words over his friend before they all trudged down the hill, depressed.

"What do we do now?" Dallas asked.

"Keep working," Clint said. "I'm going to work with the two lawmen to find out who killed him. After that we can decide what to do about the mine."

"Like sell it?" Jud asked.

"That's a possibility," Clint said, "but not something Ike would ever consider. We'll have to talk about it."

When they reached the camp, Clint watched the men scatter to go back to work. Then he headed for the mercantile for his meeting with the lawmen.

When Clint reached the mercantile, Trooper Craig was in front. Marshal Casey had not yet arrived.

"You got him buried already?" Craig asked. "That was fast."

"I didn't want him to end up on boot hill," Clint said. "What have you been doing?"

"Asking questions."

"Any good answers?"

"I'm afraid not."

They both saw Marshal Casey approaching. The tall man didn't look happy.

"What have you been up to?" Clint asked.

"Asking questions."

"Same as me," Craig said.

"Any answers?" Clint asked.

"None."

"Like me," Craig said.

Clint explained that he had already buried Ike.

"Wow," Casey said, "I hope I have a friend who gets me in the ground that fast. I hate the thought of my body lying around for people to gape at."

"I'm sure one of us can take care of that," Clint said, looking at Craig.

"He said a friend," Craig commented.

"We need to rent some tents so we can get in out of the rain," Casey said.

They went into the mercantile together.

"I spoke with Bent Miller," Craig said.

"About the girl? Or Ike Daly?" Craig asked.

"Both," Casey said.

"What did he have to say?" Clint asked.

"He's sorry," Casey said.

"Sorry he killed them?" Clint asked. "That'd be very helpful."

"No, he's just sorry to hear that they're dead."

"What did he say about the girl in Skagway?" Craig asked.

"Her name was Frankie," Clint said.

"Yes, sorry," Craig said. "What did he say about Frankie and his reputation for brutalizing whores?"

"He said he didn't know her, and he's only slapped a few whores around. He says that's not brutalizing them, it's just keeping them in line."

"Did he actually say that?" Craig asked.

"Yes," Casey said. "Apparently he grew up watching his father keep his mother in line."

"None of the whores remembers seeing him around last night?" Clint asked.

"Well," Craig said, "my questions didn't specify Bent Miller."

"Fine," Clint said, "I'll have to go and ask again."

"We'll continue to ask questions around town," Craig said.

"You can do that," Casey said. "I'll hit some of the gold camps."

"All right," Craig said, "then all that remains is to set up our tents."

"You two do that," Clint said. "I'll get started talking to the girls again. And I might have a talk myself with Bent Miller."

"Adams," Casey said as Clint turned to leave.

Clint looked at him.

"This has to be done within the letter of the law," Casey said.

"Oh, sure."

"We're serious," Craig said. "Don't kill Bent Miller."

"I won't, if he doesn't force me into it."

"And, of course," Casey said, "don't get killed."

"I don't intend to do either," Clint said. "See you gents later."

As he walked away, Casey said to Craig, "He's gonna kill him."

"I don't think so," the trooper said.

Casey looked at him.

"Unless he's sure Miller did it," Craig added.

THIRTY-EIGHT

The two lawmen picked out a tent each rather than share one. They had shared too many small campfires during their ride from Skagway to Forty Mile.

After that they found a clearing outside of town where they could set the tents up. They did so in the rain, then went inside to change into drier clothes. When they came out, Craig was still wearing his red uniform tunic.

"How many of those do you have?" Casey asked.

"Enough."

"Okay," Casey said, looking up at the sky, "now if it would only stop raining."

"Preferably before the temperature drops any more," Craig said, "or we're going to be knee-deep in snow."

"Probably a good thing Adams got his friend planted before then," Casey said.

"I'm going to walk around town and talk to people," Craig said.

"I'll hit the mines, see what the miners have to say," Casey said. "And maybe check on Miller to be sure Adams didn't kill him."

"Is Mr. Adams as fast as his reputation says?" Craig asked. "Because Bent Miller is supposed to be extremely fast."

"Well," Casey said, "my money would be on Adams."

"Miller's younger."

"Still . . ."

"It would be interesting," Craig said. "I've never really seen an Old West shoot-out."

"Would you care to make it more interesting?" Casey asked.

"How do you mean?"

"I mean a small wager."

"On who would kill who?"

Casey nodded.

"That's barbaric!"

"Like I said," Casey replied, "I'm just trying to make it a little more interesting."

Craig thought a moment, then asked, "How much more interesting?"

"Come on," Casey said, "I'll walk you to town and we can talk about it."

"Mind you," Craig said as they walked, "I'm not condoning this sort of thing . . ."

THIRTY-NINE

Clint went and talked to the whores again. This time they were all awake and dressed, and they all offered him a poke at a reduced price. At first, he tried to turn them down without insulting them. In the end, he simply told them he was too upset about his friend's death.

"I can help you deal with that, sweetie," a girl named Simone told him. She had long black hair and was very slender, with an almost flat chest. Not his type at all.

"I'm sure you could," he said. "But I just need you to answer some questions."

"Sure, come on in."

He entered her tent, found that it was not as stuffy as most of the others were.

"I air it out," she said, "after each customer. Open the back flap, and the front, let the cold air run through. I don't like trying to sleep with the smell of my work in the air."

"I can understand that," Clint said.

She sat on her cot and crossed her legs. Most of the other girls were dressed, but this one was still in a dressing gown. It split, showing her very long, slender legs. They were probably her best feature.

"Simone, do you know what Bent Miller looks like?"

"I do."

"How?"

"I used to see him around Skagway."

"When did you come up from Skagway?"

"About a month before you did."

"Has he been here to visit you?"

"No," she said.

"Why not?"

"The reason I came up here is that I could work for myself," she said, "and not for a madam, like down in Skagway. That means I get to pick and choose my own customers. I don't want him as a customer."

"Why not?"

"He likes to hit women," Simone said. "I don't like to get hit."

"So you know girls he's hit?"

"I know a girl that crazy man tried to kill," she said. "That's not gonna happen to me."

"Did you see him around the tents last night?" Clint asked.

"No."

"Did you hear anything last night?"

"You hear a lot along here," she said. "All kinds of shouting and yelling."

"What about violence?" he asked.

"Yeah, you hear that, too."

"Any last night?"

"No."

"Have you talked to any lawmen about Bent Miller?"

"The handsome one in the red tunic," she said. "I offered him a poke. He turned me down, too, like you did. But I think for a different reason."

"Like what?"

"Like I scared the poor boy," she answered with a laugh.

"Okay," Clint said. "If you remember anything, will you try to find me and let me know?"

"Sure thing," she said. "And if you change your mind about that poke, you know where to find me." She let her gown slip even more, showing leg and thigh.

"I'll remember that," he said. "Thanks, Simone."

"Sure thing, honey."

She walked to the tent flap with him and watched him walk away.

Trooper Craig questioned as many people as he could find. The problem was it was early, and the miners were working. That left him with merchants, gamblers, and other miscreants to question, if they didn't run when they saw him coming.

He ended up in the saloon, talking to one of the bartenders.

"Last night?" the barman asked. "It was crowded in here, but I do recall seeing Miller and his boss."

"Hector Tailor?"

"If that's his name. I know most people by sight."

"But you know Bent Miller?"

"Every bartender knows Miller," the man said.

"And he was here last night?"

"Yeah."

"All night?"

"I dunno that," he said. "I saw him at the bar several times, served him beers. After that he just melted into the crowd."

"So he could have left and come back."

"I suppose."

"Okay, thanks."

"Beer? On the house?"

"Not right now."

As the trooper left, the bartender—whose name was Pete—realized this was the first lawman who had ever turned down a free drink.

FORTY

Marshal Casey went up to the various mines, talked to a lot of the miners about Ike Daly and Bent Miller. He also asked when they had last been to Skagway, and to a man, they hadn't been back down there in months. Not since they started digging for gold. Casey believed them.

Casey decided to go next to the Calvin Parker camp, and see Bent Miller and his boss.

Rohm and Stash stared out at the river as it rushed by.

"You think we oughtta tell Bent what we did?" Stash asked.

"No," Rohm said.

"But he probably won't care."

"Tailor will care," Rohm said. "And Bent will have to tell him."

"You think so?"

"Tailor is his boss."

"Bent Miller don't care about a boss."

"Who's that?" Stash asked,

"Where?" Rohm asked.

Rohm turned and saw the man coming up the bank.

"Shit," he said, "that's Clint Adams."

"Relax," Stash said. "He ain't comin' for us. Just relax."

The two men stood their ground and waited.

Clint approached the two men, noticed that they were armed and watching him intently. He remembered seeing them in Skagway. They were Bent Miller's men.

"Afternoon," Clint said.

"Afternoon," Stash said. "Help ya?"

"I'm looking for Bent Miller," Clint said, "or failing that, Hector Tailor."

"Well, we don't know where Bent is right now," Stash said, "but Mr. Tailor's over in his tent."

"Which one?"

"The biggest one."

That figured.

"Okay, much obliged."

Clint walked up the slope away from the two men toward the large tent.

"Hello, inside!" he yelled.

"Come on in," a voice called out.

Clint entered, was impressed with the interior of the tent. It was warm, roomy, had a large table in the center. Hector Tailor was standing at the table, and there were plans spread out across.

"Mr. Adams," he said. Clint noticed that he rolled up a particular set of papers, as if he didn't want Clint to see them.

"What can I do for you?" Hector asked.

"I was actually looking for Bent Miller," Clint said, "but in his absence I'll talk to you."

"About what?"

"Well, two murders, really."

"Murders?"

"Yes," Clint said, "one in Skagway and one here, just last night."

"Who was killed last night?"

"My partner, Ike Daly."

"Oh no," Hector said. "How?"

"He was stabbed from behind," Clint said. "Looks like he was robbed."

"Looks like?"

"Well, yes," Clint said. "It appears he was robbed, but that might not be the reason he was killed."

"Why else would he have been killed?"

"I don't know," Clint said. "I'm looking into it, and so are the two lawmen who arrived here this morning."

"Two lawmen?"

"Yes, a U.S. marshal and a trooper from the Royal Canadian Mounties. They both rode in today, from Skagway."

"They rode in from Skagway?"

"Yes," Clint said. "A girl was killed there, as well."

"A girl?" Hector said. "One of the whores?"

"As a matter of fact, yes."

"And they rode all the way here just to find out who killed a whore?"

"A girl," Clint said. "A person. And they want to know who killed her. So do I."

"Why look for Miller?"

"Because he was the last man with her. And because he has a reputation."

"If that was a reason to suspect someone, then you would be suspected, as well."

"I don't have the same kind of reputation he has," Clint said.

"As a gunman?"

"As a man who beats women."

"And so what makes him a suspect in the killing of Daly?"

"Well, for one thing," Clint said, "Ike was competition, wasn't he?"

"For what?"

"For gold."

"Well, we're all competing for that."

"Yes," Clint said, "but I just realized how your claim and Ike's butt up against each other."

"Is that right?"

"Well, you know that," Clint said. "I'll bet that set of plans you're hiding from me shows that."

Hector went pale and asked, "What plans?"

"The ones you rolled up when I walked in," Clint said. "Mind if I see them?"

"Um," Hector said, "yes, I do mind, actually. You have no right."

"I could force you to show them to me."

Hector's eyes flicked all over the tent, as if he was looking for help, or for somewhere to run.

"And if Bent Miller killed Ike, I'm willing to bet it's because you told him to."

"You're—you're crazy."

"Then show the plans to me."

"N-No."

"Then I'll just take them off you."

As Clint approached Hector, the man backed away and began shouting, "Help! Help! Bent!"

Marshal Casey was walking up to the Parker mine as the shouting began to come from the big tent. He didn't know what was amiss, but he started running toward the tent.

Stash and Rohm heard the shouting, knew it was their boss yelling for help.

"What should we do?" Rohm asked.

"Nothin'," Stash said. "Look there."

They saw another man running toward the tents, a man wearing a gun and a badge.

"What's happenin'?" Rohm wondered.

"I don't know, but it ain't our business," Stash said. "Helping him would be up to Bent, and he's not around."

"So we just stand here?" Rohm asked.

"No," Stash said. "We get out of here."

FORTY-ONE

Marshal Casey ran into the tent as Clint wrested the plans away from Hector Tailor.

"What's goin' on?" Casey demanded.

"Marshal, arrest that man," Hector said. "He attacked me!"

"Adams?"

Clint ignored them both. He unrolled the plans and looked at them.

"Stop him!" Hector shouted.

"Shut up!" Casey ordered. "What's goin' on?" he asked Clint.

"Look at these," Clint said.

"What are they?"

Clint showed him.

"It's a set of plans for the Parker Mining Company to absorb Ike Daly's claim."

Casey looked at the plans. He couldn't make heads

or tails of them, but he could see what Clint was talking about.

"And the only way Hector here could have drawn these up was if he knew that Ike was going to be dead."

Casey looked at Hector Tailor.

"What about it?"

"He's—he's crazy."

"Well, here are the plans, Mr. Tailor," Casey said. "Did you have Bent Miller kill Ike Daly?"

"I'm—I'm only doing what Mr. Parker told me to do."

"Parker's not here," Clint said, "and you're going to blame him?"

"You—you'll have to talk to Bent," Hector said. "If he did it, he did it on his own. I never told him to kill anyone."

"I don't believe you, Hector," Clint said. "But I can't prove it."

"Then you can't arrest me!" Hector said to Casey.

"If I arrested you," Casey said, "I'd have no place to hold you."

"Then you have to let me go,"

"Or," Casey said, "I could just kill you."

Hector's eyes went wide.

"You can't do that to me!" he exclaimed. "You're the law."

Casey looked at Clint.

"We'll have to find Miller," he said, "and the trooper."

"And Miller's men!" Hector said. The more suspects he could give them, the better.

"His men?"

"He brought two men with him," Clint said. "They were outside."

"Let's go talk to them," Casey said. He looked at Hector. "Don't try to go anywhere, Mr. Tailor."

"Where could I go?" Hector said.

"If you try to leave town, you'll die out there," Casey said. "Keep that in mind."

Clint and Casey left the tent, and took the plans with them.

"Where are those other two men?" Casey asked.

"They were down there by the river," Clint said.

"Then I saw them when I got here, but they're gone now."

"They went to warn Miller," Clint said.

"Then we have to find them, and him."

"And the trooper."

"Back to town then, I guess."

FORTY-TWO

Stash and Rohm ran into Bent Miller on his way back to camp.

"Better not go there," Stash said.

"Why not?"

"Clint Adams and that marshal, they been in with Tailor."

"They see his new plans?"

"Probably."

"Shit."

"We didn't know about the lawmen," Rohm said. "Or we wouldn't have—"

"Wouldn't have what?" Bent asked.

"Shut up!" Stash told him.

Bent studied both of them.

"You two killed Ike Daly."

"I did," Stash said.

"What about you?" Bent asked,

"I was there," Rohm said, "but somebody choked me out from behind."

Jesus, Bent thought. He hadn't even recognized him when he choked him out.

"So I had to kill him alone," Stash said.

"I was on my way to kill him myself," Bent said.

The two men exchanged a glance.

"So we did the right thing," Stash said.

Miller smacked Stash and then Rohm across the mouth. Both men staggered back.

"You weren't supposed to do anything until you were told," he said.

"So what do we do now?" Rohm said.

"We've got to take care of the lawmen," Bent said, "and then Adams."

"And then what?"

"Then we'll kill Hector and take over both mines."

"And be rich."

"Yeah, I suppose," Bent said. "Not somethin' I've always wanted, but I think we're locked in now."

"So what do we do first?" Rohm asked.

"Adams and that marshal are together?"

"Yeah," Stash said.

"Then we find that trooper."

Rohm laughed. "Shouldn't be too hard to find that fella in his red coat."

FORTY-THREE

Clint and Casey were entering town when they heard the shots.

"Where?" Casey asked, looking around.

"This way," Clint said.

They ran toward the saloon, but even before they reached it, they saw the red in the street.

"Damn it!" Casey shouted.

When they reached the trooper, he was dead. He had three bullets in his chest.

The rain had stopped.

Clint and Casey stood looking down at the young Mountie.

"Where do you think they went?" Casey asked.

"I don't think they're hiding," Clint said.

"You mean?"

"In the saloon?"

"Yep."

"I'll go around back," Casey said. He looked down at the dead Mountie. "Give me five minutes."

Clint nodded.

Inside the saloon, Bent Miller, Stash, and Rohm were standing at the bar with beers. The bartender stood rigid behind the bar, afraid to move.

"Think this is smart?" Rohm asked. "Just waitin' here?"

"Better than walkin' around lookin' for them," Bent said. "When they come in, you two take the marshal. Adams is mine."

"You can have him," Stash said with feeling.

Clint waited the five minutes, then went in the front door. He saw the three men standing at the bar.

"Adams," Bent Miller said. "Welcome."

"It's all over, Bent," Clint said. "You and your boys might as well put your guns down."

"Not a chance, Adams," Bent said.

"Then I'm going to kill you for killing Ike Daly."

"What about the trooper?" Miller asked.

"I'm gonna kill you for that one," Marshal Casey said from the back of the room.

Bent, Rohm, and Stash turned to look at the lawman.

"And what about the girl?" Bent asked.

"We're going to throw her in for free," Clint said.

Clint saw the two men, Rohm and Stash, turn to face the marshal. Bent Miller turned to face him.

Casey kept his eyes on the three men, noticed what Clint had noticed. The other two men had turned to face him.

"Why'd you kill the kid?" he asked. "The trooper."

"Because it was easy," Bent said. "First the trooper, then you two."

"And after that?" Casey asked. "You guys get rich, huh?"

"That's right," Stash said. "We take over both mines."

"You forget one thing," Clint said.

"What's that?" Rohm asked without looking at him.

"Ike Daly was my partner," Clint said. "That mine is mine."

"In a few minutes," Bent Miller said, "that ain't gonna matter."

Clint looked at Bent and said, "Well then, why wait?"

He drew his gun.

FORTY-FOUR

Bent Miller didn't wait. In a split second he saw that Clint Adams was faster than he'd ever be. He vaulted over the bar as Clint fired.

Rohm and Stash heard the first shot and drew their guns. Marshal Casey drew his gun and fired calmly while Rohm and Stash got off hurried shots.

As Miller jumped over the bar, the bartender ran out from behind it, over to Clint.

"What's that bar made of?" Clint asked.

"Hardly nothin'," the bartender said. "Flimsy as hell."

"Okay," Clint said. "Get out."

The bartender ran off.

Casey fired twice as Rohm and Stash's shots flew past him on all sides. One bullet hit Rohm in the chest, and the other struck Stash in the forehead. Both men went down hard.

Clint and Casey met in the middle of the room.

"Where's Miller?" Casey asked.

"Behind the bar."

"Shall we?"

They raised their guns and emptied them into the bar. There was always a chance they missed, but when Bent Miller stood up, there was blood coming out of his mouth. Then he slumped facedown over it.

Clint and Casey walked out, stopped when they got to the trooper's body. People had gathered around to see what was happening, but it was still a sparse crowd. The miners were in the mines.

"What now?" Casey asked.

"I'm going to find somebody to run the mine for me so I can get out of Alaska. It's too damn cold."

"What about Hector?"

"By himself, he's not a threat to anyone. He'll probably quit and go back to Skagway—or disappear. Parker'll have to find someone else to do his dirty work."

"Want to ride?" Casey asked.

"Why not? I hated coming in on that pole boat."

"I'm sure the trooper would want you to have his horse."

"Did you fellas talk on the way here?"

"Sure."

"He got any family? Wife? Kids?"

"Nobody," Casey said. "Said the law was his life."

"Yeah . . ."

"We got to bury him before we go," Casey said. "Someplace nice."

Clint looked at Marshal Casey and said, "I think I know just the place."

Watch for

FRATERNITY OF THE GUN

370th novel in the exciting GUNSMITH series
from Jove

Coming in October!

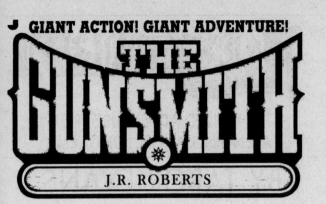

GIANT ACTION! GIANT ADVENTURE!

THE GUNSMITH

J.R. ROBERTS

LONGARM

GIANT-SIZED ADVENTURE FROM AVENGING ANGEL LONGARM.

BY TABOR EVANS

2006 Giant Edition:

LONGARM AND THE OUTLAW EMPRESS

2007 Giant Edition:

LONGARM AND THE GOLDEN EAGLE SHOOT-OUT

2008 Giant Edition:

LONGARM AND THE VALLEY OF SKULLS

2009 Giant Edition:

LONGARM AND THE LONE STAR TRACKDOWN

2010 Giant Edition:

LONGARM AND THE RAILROAD WAR

penguin.com/actionwesterns

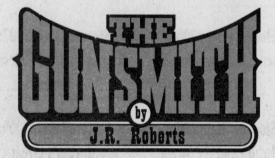